Five August Days

Hester Burton

Five August Days

Illustrated by Trevor Ridley

Oxford University Press

Oxford New York Toronto Melbourne

Oxford University Press, Walton Street, Oxford OX2 6DP

Oxford London Glasgow
New York Toronto Melbourne Auckland
Kuala Lumpur Singapore Hong Kong Tokyo
Delhi Bombay Calcutta Madras Karachi
Nairobi Dar es Salaam Cape Town

and associated companies in
Beirut Berlin Ibadan Mexico City Nicosia

Oxford is a trade mark of Oxford University Press

©Hester Burton 1981
First published 1981
Reprinted 1983

British Library Cataloguing in Publication Data
Burton, Hester
Five August days.
I. Title
823'.9'1J   80-41557
ISBN 0-19-271454-6

Photoset in Great Britain by
Rowland Phototypesetting Limited
Bury St Edmunds, Suffolk
and printed in Hong Kong

Contents

For Helen

I
The Maltings

WELL, Dan, we've got a surprise for you,' said his grandmother, when he had finished the last slice of bread and butter on the plate.

'It's only an idea,' his grandfather corrected her. 'If you don't like it you can just say so.'

'What is it?' he asked.

'We wondered if you would like to sleep out of doors.'

'What? Out in the garden?'

'In the summer-house,' his grandfather explained. 'Rose has made you up my old army camp-bed.'

As Dan got used to the idea he felt a lump coming up in his throat. They had understood. They had guessed the pain and panic that had kept pouncing out on him all the way down in the train.

'I'd like it,' he said hurriedly.

'We'll leave the front door unlocked,' said his grandmother. 'So that if you change your mind in the middle of the night you can just slip in and up to your old room. The bed's all ready for you. The one by the window. That's the one you had last year, isn't it?'

Dan nodded his head.

'I'll like it in the summer-house,' he repeated quickly. 'I'll like it very much.'

Then, in defiance of the good manners that one ought to show when staying alone with one's grandparents, he cut a large slice of fruit cake for himself and stuffed it into his mouth. He knew that if he did not start eating he would burst into tears. Nick's bed was still there in the room that they had shared last summer; and it looked just as he had known it would look: flat and white and faceless as a tomb in a churchyard.

Since Nick's death, Dan's dreams had been nightmares. Yet that first night in the quiet garden, he stirred in his sleep and smiled. In his dream he was sitting on a golden shore in the Pacific watching the sand all about him dimpling up into little mounds and the scaly heads of hundreds of baby turtles poking their way up into the warm air. He was filled with delight. He could smell the freshness of the air, hear the sighing of the wind in the palm trees behind him and feel its cool touch on his cheek.

'I'm here!' he thought. 'I'm really here!'

Every way he looked along the narrow strand, the shore was heaving with life as the little creatures struggled up out of the sand and began plodding towards the water. And now, as he watched, the first members of this tremendous hatch were paddling through the lazy waves towards the open sea. It was magic to him that he, Daniel Hassall, of 39 Elms Road, South Kensington, London, W.8., should be sitting here on a desert island actually seeing this wonder of the world with his own eyes.

Then he looked out to sea and saw Nick.

His brother was some fifty yards out from the shore, swimming strongly parallel with the coast and stopping every now and then to wave and shout back at him. Dan was glad that he was out there fooling about in the Pacific, for nothing splendid and happy was quite complete without Nick. In his dream he could see the grin on his freckled face and the water glistening on his upraised arm. By this time, the first of the baby turtles to take to the sea had almost reached him and, as Dan watched, he saw Nick lunge towards the nearest creature, catch it up out of the wave, and hurl it back towards the shore.

His brother's shriek of laughter woke him up.

A long crack of grey light stretched low across the western sky. In the darkness it was raining. He could hear the drops falling through the birch tree close beside his camp-bed. As he lay and listened to the night, a boy laughed again in the village street on the other side of the garden wall. The old, old misery of waking swept over him afresh. Nick, for all his laughing, was still stone dead. As for himself, he was not on a South Sea island after all. He was in Suffolk. At Danescourt. In his grandparents' summer-house. While he sat up in bed watching the soft veils of rain sweeping across the tennis lawn in the dim summer night, a light went on in his grandparents' bedroom. If they were going to bed then it must be still quite early, not more than half-past ten, perhaps. He had hours and hours of darkness still to get through. Someone inside the bedroom drew the curtain across the window, shutting in the light.

'I'm on my own here at Danestone,' he thought wretchedly. 'Entirely on my own.'

Two counties to the west and more than a hundred miles away, another boy was finding himself in a far more dreadful plight.

He stood in the pitch darkness of the shed, his heart hammering like the drums at the disco and his breath heaving in and out of him in huge, uncontrollable sobs, for he had run away from the break-in faster than he thought anyone could possibly run.

'I'm another Sebastian Coe,' flashed through his mind. And, despite the police-hunt closing in on him, he wanted to laugh. 'Might've been everyone's hero, if only I'd known.'

The shed smelt of rabbits' urine, a smell that took him back to his childhood.

'Poor devils, shut up here in their own stink year after year,' he thought as he heard one of the creatures nuzzling against the wire of its cage.

His breath was coming more quietly now. He would wait half a minute longer and then he would slip out of the back of the shed and over the garden walls and back to the parking lot behind The Six Bells and the car whose keys he had stolen. Once behind the wheel, he would be out of Higham Ferrers in no time at all. Take the Kettering road, if he liked. Or west to Northampton. Or east to St Neots. Make for Bedford? No. He would keep out of Bedford. He did not like Bedford. Once he was out of their patch, the police would surely not follow him farther, not just for ten Mars Bars and the handful of coppers the old woman had left in her till?

And then he heard it: the footfall on the garden path.

He froze where he stood.

'Come out, Kevin. We've got you.'

The voice was startlingly close – not twenty feet away. The steps grew closer. Through a crack in the shed door, the boy could see a thickening in the darkness. Frightened though he was, he kept his head and listened hard. The fool, he thought. There was only one of them.

The steps came on. The single policeman was now barely a yard from the door.

'Keep away,' he shrieked at last. 'I've got a gun.'

The thickening in the darkness removed itself.

'Don't be a fool. Throw it down and come out.'

The fuzz was standing inches away on the other side of the shed wall.

The boy held the gun in his hand. He had his finger on the trigger.

'Come in and get me,' he taunted.

'Throw down the gun.'

The boy looked back through the shed to make sure of his exit. The half-door into the back garden was ajar. Then he groped about with his left hand and came upon a garden trowel hanging neatly from a hook.

'All right. You've got me. There's the gun,' he shouted.

And he threw the trowel hard on the concrete floor.

The young policeman rushed the door, wrenched it open, and received the full blast of the explosion in his face. For full measure, the boy kicked him hard in the groin.

Then he fled.

Half an hour later, he was across the River Ouse at St Neots and heading east. It was not good to look back on what he had done. So he shut it out; kept his eyes on the road and the hedges and trees. That was what was important. To eat up the miles. To get away. To lose oneself. To lie up somewhere till one could turn oneself into somebody else. But first he must ditch this white Allegro; he must ditch it quickly and find another. The Six Bells would be closing in a matter of minutes, and the man would come out and find his car gone. He must hide the old bus in some woods; push it into a pond; over a cliff – anything as long as when they found it he'd be a long way away, eating up the miles in something else. The flat land on either side put him in a panic. There was no cover here, no cover at all, not for a boy who'd done what he'd done to that policeman.

Before he knew it, he was three miles along the new Cambridge by-pass, with the city lights paling the clouds in the southern sky.

'There's not a hope of an exchange on a by-pass,' he thought with alarm. 'And like as not they'll have police-checks out on a road like this.'

He took the next turn into the city. There he

had the devil's luck. It was nearly midnight and the streets were deserted of everything save parked cars. In a new estate in the first suburb he found two white Allegros drawn up at the curb. He parked his own between them, walked half a mile down the road, and then nicked a Suzuki out of a front garden and pushed it quietly away.

An hour later, he was racing along byways in the direction of Eye in Suffolk. He had no idea where he was making for. But that did not matter. He had escaped. He was free. He was laughing into the wind at the cleverness of it all.

Next morning, back in Danestone, Dan woke early to the unaccustomed light and sat up and looked about him in surprise. He had never slept outside before; never seen the dawn. In fact, as he gazed across the garden in the pearly greyness, he wondered whether this *was* the dawn or some even more remote beginning to a summer's day that no one had ever told him about. Blackbirds and thrushes were pecking for worms in the grass, their feet sending up little spurts of water as they hopped about on the rain-soaked lawn. Save for the calling of the birds, the silence was profound. No one was awake – not even the flowers; the poppies and the daisy-like things in his grandmother's border were shut up tight. But it was the light that astonished him most. Nothing was quite the right colour, neither his grandparents' house nor the roses climbing up the wall nor the tops of the orchard trees nor the bed of petunias close at hand. It was as though he were looking at everything through a kind of gauze. Then he wondered if this were some strange trick of his peculiar eyesight, and he groped about for his glasses on the chair beside his camp bed. But, even with his glasses on, the garden looked ghostly and new. He looked at his watch. It was half-past five. This too was astonishing. He had never been awake at half-past five before.

He thought about this for a little. His grandparents would go on sleeping for hours and hours.

Then slowly he smiled. It was now or never. Danestone lay open before him. He could get up and visit its secret places entirely on his own. He swung his legs over the side of the bed, put on his school mackintosh and tucked his pyjama legs into the tops of his Wellington boots and stepped out into the grey light.

'I owe it to Nick,' he told himself, as he walked across the wet tennis lawn. 'He'll want to know if everything's the same as last year.'

He considered that he also owed it to himself, and as he passed the edge of his grandfather's rock-garden he first glanced furtively all round and then heaved up one of the jutting-up stones and peered underneath. Yes. The wood-lice were still there . . . and they still rolled themselves up into frightened balls; and the slimy, snaily smell that came up from underneath the stone was still there, too.

'Come on. Come *on*!' Nick seemed to urge him. 'No one's interested in your disgusting bugs. It's the maltings . . . the *maltings* we want to see.'

Their grandparents' house, and the summer-house where Dan had slept, were immediately behind a high brick wall which bordered the village street. But the garden extended well back into the Suffolk marsh, becoming a much more secluded and private affair. On one side, tall cedars and chestnut trees shut it off from a grassy lane leading from the street to the maltings, and it stretched through rose-garden and orchard, and beyond, until finally it merged with the marsh in a boggy jungle of nettles and willows. It was through the nettles and over an iron railing that one came to the back of the forbidden place.

Yes, the maltings were forbidden all right.

'Remember, Dan, you're to keep out of them,' his grandfather had told him last night. 'They're dangerous. Mr Fenton ought to have boarded them up years ago.'

It had been bad enough last year, he had explained, with the village boys larking about in the derelict buildings; but it was worse now. During the winter gales one of the beams near the roof had caved in.

'We'll have a tragedy on our hands one of these days. The whole place will come tumbling about some fool's head. So don't go into them, Dan. For you, they're out of bounds.'

As Dan trailed off through the orchard, he trod squelch on a fallen apple.

'Well, there's no harm in just *looking* at the place,' he muttered. 'I'll just sit on the railings and stare straight ahead of me. No one could blame me for that.'

So he pushed his way through the tall nettles and stooped under the low branches of the silver willows and came to the end of the garden, where the railings and the gaunt row of dead elms fenced in the higher ground. Beyond stretched the malt-ings, long and low and dark against the silent marsh, their quaint chimney rising like a battered pagoda in the strange early light.

The sight of the place gave him a terrible ache for last summer, for it had been their secret kingdom – Nick's and his – made all the more precious to them because it had been forbidden. On one of the malting-house floors they had built a fort of rotting timbers and mouldy slabs of cattle-cake and old sacks that had once contained the sprouting barley. It was here that they had taken the raspberries and plums they had stolen from the garden; and it was here that they had hidden from their cousins and all the other unwanted visitors to their grandparents' house.

Now, seeing the rambling old building once again, he felt such a stab of love and longing that there was no help for it but that he should climb over the railings and wade through the towering hogweeds towards it.

'I'll go round to the dike,' he told himself, 'and look up at the gantry. There's no harm in that.'

Long ago, even before his mother could remember, the black-sailed wherries had sailed up the Danestone dike from the River Waveney with their holds full of barley. The heavy sacks had been hauled up from the wharf by the stout hook and chain that hung from the cabin under the malting roof and had then been swung up into the upper floor. Nick had once tried to make the cogwheel work, but the machinery had been jammed with rust.

As Dan approached the front of the maltings, the swish of the bending hogweeds sounded so loud in the grey stillness that he was suddenly swept with the enormity of what he was doing. He was disobeying his grandfather. He was trespassing. And he was doing it all in his pyjamas. What if someone else were about as early as himself?

As if in answer, just as he was rounding the corner and looking down on the dike, his guilt seemed to explode all about him. An appalling clattering shook the air, as though every tile on the crazy maltings were falling to the ground. He clutched at the wall in panic. Then he saw the wild duck flying up into the air and whirring away over the reed tops.

He stood quite still, waiting for the morning to settle. Then, his heart still thumping from his fright, he slipped quickly through the maltings door and into the shadowy coolness of last summer's secret world.

Lying on the tiled floor of the drying chamber under the heap of rotten sacks, Kevin Britton woke up to the clattering of the birds.

'Christ!' he muttered, 'Where the hell've I got myself now?'

He looked up at the huge funnel of the chimney over his head and saw the grey eye of the dawn. Then he gazed at the rafters stretching away over the topmost malting-house floor. Was it an old, ruined chapel into which he had stumbled last night? No, it was more like a warehouse or somebody's crazy old barn. He remembered that he had been glad of it in the darkness and that, once inside, he had fumbled about him and then climbed and climbed and climbed. He could see now the topmost rungs of the ladder that had brought him to where he was.

Suddenly his whole body froze. There was a noise far below him. Quite a little noise – but stealthy. It was not a mouse; not a rat. He strained his ears. There was someone moving quietly about three floors down.

Silently, he reached under the sacks for his gun.

Far below, on the ground floor, Dan was finding the maltings as musty and reassuring as Danestone parish church. He at once felt at home, for here round the entrance everything was just as it had been before. The weighing scales were still rusting away near the door; the wooden shovels still hung from their pegs on the wall; behind the maltster's table, the rack for the samples was still stuffed with the mouldering small bags of grain. Not a thing seemed to have changed. As he groped his way through the dim light towards the furnace house, even the smell was the same. He remembered now that whenever it rained the iron of the rusting furnace gave off a strong, wet, metally smell, which would have been horrible if one had met it anywhere else but here. This morning the stench was so strong that he seemed to taste it in his mouth. He kicked the cold clinkers still spewed out over the brick floor and came upon the old riddling-iron which he and Nick had once thought to lug upstairs to their fort. Nothing had changed. Everything was just as they had left it last summer.

Then he climbed the rough, worn stairs to the upper floor and saw at once how wrong he had been. As his grandfather had said, one of the beams under the roof had caved in. Splintered wood and red pantiles had poured down on their fort, burying it under a mournful pile of rubbish. Above gaped the sky. Feeling a lump in his throat, he turned his back on it. He could not bear to look at where they had played.

Gazing heartsick down the length of this upper floor, he saw that the light outside the barred windows was growing stronger. Far away the sun must have risen over the rim of the North Sea. He must not stay here much longer. He must get back to his bed before anyone woke up. And yet, he hated to hurry away, for he felt Nick was still here. He felt him everywhere about him.

At the far end of the shadowy gallery he saw the ladder that led up to the drying-floor. The drying-floor was immediately over the furnace and had strangely beautiful pricked tiles that let through the heat. He would take one look – just one last look – at the tiles and the place where he and Nick had once lit a fire, and then he would be off back to bed and never come here again.

The wood of the ladder was rotten. He knew that it was rotten. Last year one of the rungs had broken under Nick's weight. So he mounted it slowly and carefully, his tongue between his teeth, and feeling his way. In this manner, when half-way up and with his shoulders level with the drying-house floor, he came eye to eye with Kevin Britton, crouched down beside his heap of sacks.

Startled almost out of his wits, he saw a boy who was almost a man.

The young thief saw a child in glasses, wearing his pyjamas.

'What the hell d'you think you're doing here?' he shouted, jumping to his feet and towering over Dan's head.

'Nothing,' gasped Dan. 'I wasn't going to do anything. Honest. I . . . I was just looking.'

He was still clinging to the ladder. He wanted to

jump straight down and run away. But he was frightened. It was a ten-foot drop.

And now it was too late. The terrifying stranger had stooped down quickly and grasped him by his two wrists.

'Looking? Looking for what?'

'Nothing,' Dan muttered, near to tears.

The boy tugged fiercely at his wrists and dragged him up on to the drying-floor.

'Don't be a fool,' he hissed. 'You don't come nosing about a place like this . . . and climbing up a ladder just looking for *nothing*.'

Once up on the drying-floor, Dan felt a little better.

'I . . . I was only looking at where we used to play.'

He knew that he looked a fool standing there in his pyjamas and his gumboots. But the fierce boy looked a fool, too. His hair was grey with barley dust and he had a smear of chocolate on his chin.

Much of the terror had gone out of Kevin, too.

'You woke me up,' he grumbled. 'It's the first good kip I've had for weeks.'

'Goodness!' Dan exclaimed looking at the heap of rotten sacks. 'Is this where you always sleep?'

Kevin looked at him guardedly and then shrugged his shoulders.

'I kip around,' he replied vaguely. 'It's better here than out under a hedge.'

'Is that what you do? Just walk about from place to place and sleep where you like?'

Kevin allowed himself a grin.

'Something like,' he replied.

But behind the grin he was thinking what to do with this awkward, inquisitive intruder. Should he knock him on the head and then make a dash for it? He looked about him. It was too late. The sun was up. There would be descriptions of him by now in all the newspapers and appeals to the public on the radio. He could not trust himself to broad daylight. He would be picked up in no time. He would have to wait till it was dark. But this child? He would run straight home and tell his family what he had found.

It was Dan himself who provided the answer.

'I must go now,' he said anxiously. 'I must get back, you see, before anybody wakes up.'

'Why?'

'Because . . . because I oughtn't to be here,' he blurted out. 'It's . . . it's out of bounds . . . these maltings.'

'*Out of bounds?*' yelped Kevin Britton. 'Christ! Have you escaped from a Remand Home?'

'Good heavens, no!' exclaimed the astonished Dan.

He was staying with his grandparents, he explained. And the maltings were dangerous. They ought to have been pulled down years ago. They were so dangerous that they might fall down any moment and kill someone. So his grandfather had made him promise not to go into them.

'And you have,' said Kevin, with a slow smile.

He looked more carefully at this child caught out in his small crime – and weighed his own chances.

'Well, I'll not tell on you,' he said, still smiling.

'At least I'll not tell on you if you'll do something for me in return.'

'What?'

'Nick off a pint of milk.'

'*Milk?*'

'That's it. I'm thirsty.'

Dan was not quite the simpleton that he looked.

'Why don't you buy it yourself?'

'I've got no money. Look.'

And Kevin pulled out the lining of the only pocket in his jacket that was empty.

Dan nodded. All right. The boy was broke.

As he climbed down the ladder he told himself that one bottle of milk was not such a dreadful thing to steal from his grandmother. Once he had brought it back to this frightening stranger he could forget all about him – put the whole affair out of his mind – and go on quietly with his Danestone holiday.

'And you'll not say that you've seen me here in the maltings,' Kevin called softly down as Dan reached the floor. 'Or you'd be giving yourself away, wouldn't you?'

Stumbling back through the hogweed, Dan blamed himself bitterly for managing things so badly. He had been a fool and a coward. And – as always – he began wondering what Nick would have thought of the way he had behaved.

Yes, you were a fool, all right, Nick whispered in his ear. *Couldn't you see the boy was quite as frightened as you were?*

'Frightened? Was he really?'

Scared stiff of you coming up that ladder. Why, you duffer, can't you see the fellow's on the run?

Dan stopped dead in his tracks, letting the tall stems settle and the marsh and his grandparents' garden steady themselves in the early morning sunlight. Not everything Nick said was true; he had learnt that in the last few months. But his brother was so often right that one believed him first and only doubted him afterwards.

On the run? From home? From school? No, the boy had looked too old for that. He had needed a shave. Besides, it was August, so there *was* no school. Had he really been frightened? But he couldn't have been. He had been so sure of himself. Besides, frightened of what? Certainly not of him – Dan – standing there in his pyjamas, stammering like an idiot. No. This was just one of Nick's stories, made up to tease him or to give him a scare.

He plodded cautiously on towards the darkened house, wondering how best to take a pint of milk without his grandmother noticing its loss.

Yet, when he came to the conservatory, he stopped dead again.

The thought crashed over his head like a thunderclap.

On the run?

If there was one person who must know what it was like to be on the run, then it was Nick.

Left on his own, Kevin Britton was even more disgusted with himself than Dan had been. Why had he not knocked the child unconscious and then gagged and trussed him . . . anything to stop him from blabbing his story to his grandfather? What a fool he had been to let him go!

'I'm so tired out,' he thought bitterly. 'I don't know what I'm doing.'

He looked longingly at his dusty bed. He was desperate for sleep. But he knew also that he must not get caught up here in this queer shelf of a room – trapped like a rat – with no way of escape. So, instead, he reached into the bed for his gun, slipped it into his empty pocket, and began climbing down the rickety ladder. He must find out where he had got himself last night – and try to plan what he should do next.

The child's grandfather was right, he thought, as he stood on the upper floor and looked about him. The whole place was crazily unsafe. The tiles round the jagged hole in the roof looked as though they would come slithering down on his head if he raised his voice; and when he peered down at his feet he caught a glimpse of the floor below through the cracks in the rotten boards. He trod more gingerly then and made for the sagging stairs. It was safer and darker on the ground floor, he found, for the brambles and nettles had grown up over the maltings' windows. Better still, there were two doors, one opening into some inner darkness, the other into the sunlight of the outdoors world.

He moved towards the light and stood on the dusty threshold, blinking at the morning. At his feet was a rotten wharf and, beyond it, a dike, weed-mantled at its head but deep and crystal clear straight ahead. On his left, a grassy lane led away between railings and a garden wall; and to his right lay a marsh that stretched miles and miles to the horizon. It was worse than his worst fears. To the left up the lane must lie a village and to the right lay a landscape without cover. He was caught in a vast cul-de-sac.

He saw that there was a tow-path along the bank on the far side of the dike and, recalling his brief passion for fishing, he realised that boys and even grown men might very soon be walking along the path with their rods. He must act quickly. He must rescue the Suzuki from the bed of nettles and get it inside, out of the glinting of the sun. As for himself, he must trust to the known danger of these tumbledown maltings and pray that the child in pyjamas was too scared of his grandfather to tell him that he had found him.

There was nothing else that he could do.

2
Henry

D AN, dear, you don't look very well,' said his grandmother anxiously as they sat at breakfast.

He was quite well, he replied hurriedly – as well, he thought, as anyone would feel who had so much on his mind.

'If you don't like sleeping out of doors, we'll quite understand,' said his grandfather, 'it was just an idea. . . .'

'I do like it. I like it very much. Honest, I do,' he said between mouthfuls of porridge. 'It's fun . . . fun watching the birds pecking for worms.'

If only he could eat with a will and seem cheerful, he thought, they'd never guess what was wrong.

For Nick had been right. The boy *was* on the run.

When he had left the stranger, Dan had slipped into the house through the front door and had stood on the mat listening to the silence upstairs. Then he had peered at the clock in the hall. Ten past six! Only forty minutes since he had woken up! Then he had groped his way into the kitchen, for it was shadowy indoors with the curtains still drawn and he had felt too guilty to turn on the lights. Silly, he thought as he moved towards the ghostly white refrigerator – for he had his story ready. A foolproof story. He had crept into the house, he could tell them, because he was hungry. It wasn't a crime to be hungry. His grandparents would understand. He had opened the refrigerator door and found that there was only one pint of milk inside.

'I can't take that,' he had thought. 'Granny'll notice it's gone straight away.'

It was while he had been standing there, wondering what to do, that he had heard the extra-ordinary sound. It was eerie . . . and mechanical . . . and, somehow, *gliding*. . . . like a spaceship coming in to land. It had filled him with terror. Something unearthly was discovering his guilt. Then there had come a rattle and a clink of glass . . . and his fright had become more mundane. Someone with heavy footsteps was approaching the back door. A moment later, bang went the milk bottles on the kitchen window-sill, and the footsteps went away. He had sighed with relief. Moreover, his problem had been solved. He had waited, listening for the milk float to glide out of hearing, and had then cautiously opened the kitchen window and taken in one of the three pints of milk. His afterthought had quite shocked him by its cleverness: he had reached out again and altered his grandmother's milk clock from 3 to 2.

It was as he had been moving on tiptoe towards the kitchen door that his brother had spoken again.

Don't be mean, Dan. Take him some food as well. I bet the poor devil's hungry.

He couldn't do that, he had protested. It would be stealing.

Nonsense. She wouldn't mind. Think how much she gives to Oxfam.

He had thought about this for a moment and had then concluded that it was really only changing one hungry person for another.

That's right. Take a loaf out of the deep freeze. She keeps so much there she's sure not to miss it.

And since Dan didn't fancy dry bread for himself, he had pulled out a half pound of butter, too, and a carton which his grandmother had labelled 'Chicken Marengo. Left over. 7.7.79'. Then, putting the loot in a plastic bag which he had found hanging on the peg on the kitchen door, he had slipped out of the house into broad daylight and returned to the maltings.

He had come upon the stranger sooner than he had expected to, sitting slouched on the old weighing-machine by the door, half-asleep. Dan's shadow must have startled him, for he had suddenly sprung to his feet, snarling like a cornered cat. Dan had dropped the plastic bag and fled.

But the boy had raced after him.

'Thanks,' he had panted as he had clutched him by the shoulder. 'Thanks a lot. I . . . I didn't think it was you.'

Looking up into his grey and hunted face, Dan had felt his heart do a somersault inside him. Had Nick looked so wretched when the port

31

authorities had been searching for him in the hold of the ship?

The boy had smiled tensely.

'I'll not let you down,' he had said. 'I'll be off tonight.'

Slowly the warmth of the kitchen and the smell of bacon and the sound of his grandmother's voice drifted back to him.

'So it would be nice, Dan, if the two of you could be friends,' she was saying.

'Friends?' he asked, bewildered.

'Yes, you and Henry.'

'Who's Henry?' he blurted out, still at sea and too tactless to hide the fact.

'I don't believe you've been listening to a word we've said.'

This was worse and worse. His grandmother sounded hurt . . . and he couldn't bear her to feel hurt. His grandfather lowered his 'Daily Telegraph' and gave them both his strange, twisted smile.

'We're only a couple of old fogies, Madge,' he said. 'When I was Dan's age I just let their talk sail over my head.'

Dan blushed uncomfortably.

'I'm very sorry,' he mumbled.

So his grandmother began again. Dan's cousins, Simon and Nigel, had brought a schoolfriend home for the holidays, and the poor boy's visit was proving an unmitigated disaster.

'Why?' he asked. He hated his cousins, and the

fact that someone else was hating them – and a schoolfriend, too – intrigued him.

'Because he doesn't know how to swim.'

'He can't *swim*?'

He saw it all in a flash. The summer holidays at Danestone were impossible if one did not know how to swim, for all the best things – like sailing and water-picnics and the Rushby Regatta – all took place on the river. It was even pointless driving over to the sea if one couldn't swim.

'Didn't they know?' he asked.

'Of course they did,' his grandfather replied scornfully. 'But the young fools somehow thought that it wouldn't matter.'

'And now,' continued his grandmother, 'the poor boy's left on his own whenever they go sailing. And it's so embarrassing for your Aunt Philippa. She doesn't really want him hanging round the house all day.'

Intrigued though he was, Dan also felt wary. All his life, it seemed to him, his parents had been trying to find friends for him, feeble, shy, flabby boys – as unlike Nick as one could imagine – and always he had found them a burden. Now, his grandparents had joined in the search, and he was to be saddled with his hateful cousins' cast-off.

'Well, you'll meet him in under an hour,' commented his grandfather, glancing at his watch. 'They're all coming over for a knock-up at tennis. So let's hope you'll take to each other.'

'He really seems a very *nice* boy,' said his grandmother as she rose to clear the table. 'I believe you'll like him.'

Dan groaned inwardly. He sloped off into the kitchen garden feeling hedged in and threatened. He was being invaded from all sides. He saw that everything about this holiday was going wrong and that it was nearly all his own fault. If only he had not disobeyed his grandfather he would never have come upon the stranger in the maltings, never stolen food from his grandmother, never felt this frightening menace. Well, he was paying for it. He was having to spend the morning with his cousins, playing tennis, and making friends with a boy whom he did not want to meet.

He grabbed himself a handful of fat pea-pods in passing and then stuffed them in his pocket. But not even the future comfort of sweet, raw peas could lift his gloom. The boy wouldn't want to know *him* either. Coming from the same school, he'd be just like his two cousins: rich, successful, and sneering. He'd just use Dan's friendship to despise him. He knew exactly how it would be. The three of them would laugh at him and call him a rabbit because he could not see well enough to hit the ball. Disconsolately, he wandered back through the house and across the lawn, taking his peas to his favourite branch up the tall cedar. He was at least private there, perched high up between the silver-green layers of the tree and – being hidden – he might perhaps think of a way out of the troubles that beset him.

But there was no way. Without Nick, he wondered if there ever *could* be a way.

Then he fell to thinking of all the things that he would have done with the morning if he'd only been left to himself. He would have mooned about the marshes and gone down to Danestone beach; then he would have come back by the village and bought himself a skein of black licorice from Mrs Mobbs, and then slipped up the backstairs to the attic where generations of his forbears had left the trophies of their travels: Australian boomerangs, cases of tropical butterflies, the two Indian wrought-silver censers with their little black cones of incense, odd, muddled-up stamp collections, drawers of strange birds' eggs nestling in cotton-wool, his grandmother's wedding-dress, old albums of photographs. He loved this junk of the past. But it was a secret, family love – not to be shared with this stranger who could not swim.

He was still perched up in his eagle's nest when he saw Rose, his grandmother's daily-woman, come out of the front door and walk across the lawn. He liked Rose. He had known her all his life. Indeed, she was almost as much a part of their Danestone holidays as their grandparents and the marsh and the river – and quite as unchanging. As she passed under the cedar, he would have liked to have called down 'Hallo', but he knew that she would stop and peer up and then start talking and talking and talking about Nick, and somehow he couldn't bear to exchange even the kindest of words about his brother with himself high up in the tree and she thirty feet below. So he let her go, watching her instead as she stopped every now and then to smell a rose or pull up a groundsel, taking her time as she wandered towards the summer-house to make his bed.

Then, almost immediately, Simon and Nigel and their friend, each armed with tennis rackets – and his cousins with their bathing things – burst through the front gate into the garden, half an hour before their time. They ran into the house shouting his name and then, a minute later, came out through the conservatory followed by their grandfather, carrying the tennis net.

'Dan, Dan, you flebster,' shouted Nigel. 'We're here. We've come to play tennis.'

Dan stayed where he was. It was their idea, not his – and they might as well get on with the job of putting up the net without his help. Besides, he wanted to try and guess what sort of boy it was that they had brought with them.

Seen from above, Henry looked a blur of reddish-brown hair and large feet. 'He looks far

too gangling and grown-up for me,' was his first thought; but then, as he watched him turn to his grandfather and with a kind of quiet authority relieve the old man of the net and tell his two friends to go back and fetch the two posts, it came to him that there might be something in him after all. Even though he couldn't swim, he wasn't just a nobody. He knew how to treat the horrible pair.

'Dan, Dan,' shouted Nigel as he struggled out with one of the posts. 'Where are you? You're wasting our time.'

'Well, what's so awful about that?' thought Dan, as he pulled one of the pea-pods out of his pocket, burst it open, and shovelled its contents into his mouth.

His grandfather, he saw, had gone back into the house to look for him, just as Rose – having made his bed – was returning across the tennis lawn.

'Rose, have *you* seen the twirp?' asked Nigel, as he banged his post into its slot.

Rose stopped dead in mid course.

'Who do you mean?' she snapped.

'Why, our cousin.'

'His name's Daniel,' she said angrily.

Simon, struggling with the post on his side of the court, burst out laughing.

'We only call him Daniel, Rose, when he's fit for nothing but the lion's den.'

'Well, I haven't seen him. And I hope you'll mend your manners before you find him. You ought to be ashamed of yourselves.'

Dan watched wonderingly as she stumped off

towards the house. He had never before seen her so angry.

As for Henry, he was stooping over the net, spread out on the lawn, trying to smooth out a kink in the wire that ran along the top.

'Well. I suppose we've got to do something about him,' said Simon, when the net was at last in place and wound up tight.

Dan ate another pod-full of peas.

'He's probably hiding,' said Nigel.

'Then we'll have to flush him out. We'll each go different ways. You stay and look for him in the garden, Henry. And you go along the tow-path,' said Simon, turning to his brother. 'I'll make sure he's not in the maltings.'

The maltings!

Dan gasped with such horror that he nearly fell out of the tree.

As his cousins ran across the orchard to the head of the dike, he scrambled down in such haste that he tore his hands and his shirt and almost fell into the arms of Henry waiting below.

'Goodness!' the boy exclaimed, laughing. 'That's where you were! I wondered why empty pea-pods were falling out of a cedar tree.'

It was a friendly, pleasant greeting from a friendly, ugly face, but Dan was too panic-stricken to respond.

'I'm here,' he yelled after his cousins. 'Stop looking for me. I'm here on the front lawn.'

The game of tennis was even worse than he had thought it would be, for the three boys from Granthams Preparatory School had been playing tennis all the past summer term while Dan had not held a racket in his hand since he and Nick had been down at Danestone last August.

'Pity they don't teach you proper games at your primary school,' Simon observed. 'But we'll have to make the best of it.'

Well, it was *he* who had to make the best of it, Dan thought bitterly – having to play with these snobs who would make fun of him . . . and having to show this boy Henry how terribly bad he was.

'Simon, you're the best of the three of us,' said Nigel, 'so why don't you take Dan as a partner? It'll be a handicap.'

Henry gave him a sudden smile, as though to say: It's only a game. It's not important. And Dan, startled into smiling back, saw bright eyes under the mop of hair, a crooked nose as though someone had bashed it in a fight, and toes coming through his sneakers. He looked surprisingly un-grand for someone who came from Granthams. Then the boy trailed off with Nigel to the other end of the court and he – Dan – was left grasping the jumble-sale tennis racket which his grandmother had bought him and praying hard that he would not disgrace himself worse than he could help.

Henry's service ball came over quite gently. He swiped it hard with the unfamiliar racket and hit it on the wood, so that it shot off sideways into the rock-garden.

'Oh bad luck,' shouted Henry.

'Jolly *good* luck, you mean,' laughed Simon. 'Last year he hardly ever managed to hit the ball at all.'

Nigel giggled.

Dan felt his glasses misting up. Then he bit his lip. This horrible game could not go on for ever. He must stick it out . . . show them he didn't care. When it was over he could take this boy with him down on the marshes . . . show him the dragonflies. They might even take a net with them and try and catch minnows. They might even. . . .

'Wake up,' bawled his partner.

And, waking up only just in time, he swiped again at the ball coming towards him and again hit it on the wood. But this time it sneaked forwards, tripped up on the net, and fell dead in Nigel's court.

'What a ruddy shot!' Nigel shouted angrily, having run forward but failed to get it up.

'Well, I got it over,' he shouted back, feeling rather pleased with himself.

'Jolly unsportsmanlike. It's not the way we play at Granthams.'

'More fools us!' exclaimed Henry unexpectedly. 'They do it quite often at Wimbledon.'

'Just think of Dan at Wimbledon,' burst out Simon, crowing with laughter.

Even Dan thought this was rather funny. He could see himself hitting balls off the wood into the referee's face – or worse still, into the royal box. Yet, though he could smile at himself, the game was still a weariness. He was so inconceivably bad, missing more balls than he hit, that his partner was now running all over the court, taking the shots that ought rightfully to have been his. Well, let him. It gave him time to listen to the sharp ping of the ball against the taut strings and the distant cackle of hens and the soft cooing of the collared doves sitting in the trees. And once, throwing a glance across the orchard at the distant maltings peering through the willows, he wondered whether the fierce boy of the early morning was standing at one of the windows watching the four of them playing their silly game. He wondered whether the loaf and the butter and the chicken stew had thawed out by now.

He felt a whistle of air by his cheek.

'For God's sake, Dan,' roared his partner. 'If you're going to play tennis do try to keep your mind on the game. Haven't you ever learnt to concentrate?'

'Of course I have,' he muttered.

He knew he was not a fool. He'd come top in maths in his form last term and he'd managed to recite the whole of 'Horatius on the Bridge' without forgetting a word.

'They don't teach them a thing at Dan's school,' Nigel remarked to Henry. 'They don't do Greek. They don't even do Latin.'

'What on earth *do* you do?' asked Simon, forgetting about tennis for the moment to join in the jeer.

'Basketwork,' sniggered Nigel.

'No we don't,' Dan burst out, beside himself with anger. He loved his school, and he could not bear to hear it being laughed at. 'We learn a lot of things that you don't learn.'

'Like knitting and making toffee?' Nigel sneered.

The blood rushed up into Dan's face. He hated his cousins. He longed for the earth to open and swallow them up. Or, better still, he longed to be able to hurl a thunderbolt at them so that it was he – Dan Hassall – who had demolished them both.

'Come on, tell us what you *do* do,' Simon urged.

Desperately – mindlessly – trying to defend everything that he loved: his school; his parents; Nick – he opened his mouth. And out of it came the incredible word '*Chinese*'.

'Yes,' he gasped. 'That's it. We learn Chinese.'

'*Chinese*?' they all exclaimed.

The four of them stood motionless on the tennis court in utter amazement. Dan felt giddy with awe. Where on earth had the word come from? Then he looked at the three prep-school boys and felt breathless with fright. For what was he to do now?

Stick it out, he decided. There was nothing else he could do.

'There's nearly a thousand million Chinese,' he gabbled, as he raked about in his mind for all that he knew about China. 'And they're very ancient and very clever. My father says they'll soon be more important than the Russians . . . so it's sensible to learn their language. Much more sensible than learning languages which nobody speaks.'

'Chinese!' exclaimed Henry again. 'Good Lord!'

'I . . . I haven't got very far yet,' Dan conceded wisely. 'We'll learn more when we get into the Comprehensive.'

'Don't think I'd like to learn Chinese,' said Nigel, dismissing the subject with contempt. 'It sounds a very un-English sort of thing to do.'

They took up their game again, all strangely subdued: three of them because the glories of Granthams seemed suddenly dimmed; the fourth because he was appalled by his thumping great lie. His father and mother hated lies. Not telling the truth was the worst crime in the family calendar.

'Well done,' cried Henry.

In his abstraction it appeared that he must have hit the ball quite well.

'You're getting a little better,' said Simon grudgingly.

But he felt no triumph. His heart was not in it.

Why hadn't his parents taken him with them to Switzerland? Why had they sent him down here for him to get himself into this terrible mess? He had disobeyed his grandfather, stolen from his grandmother, and now he had told a most idiotic lie. How on earth was he to get out of it all?

'Well done,' cried Henry again. 'You're getting much better. That last shot's won you the game.'

Dan looked across the net at the friendly, smiling boy and felt sick. When Henry found out what a lie he had told he would despise him for ever more.

But something more quickly shaming now burst over his head.

'Whose service is it now?' asked Nigel.

'Mine,' claimed Simon.

'No, it isn't,' Henry protested. 'It's Dan's.'

Now he came to think of it, they'd played three games at least and he hadn't yet served.

'Yes, it's mine,' he said.

Then he gasped – for he knew in an instant what he had done.

'Moin! Moin! Moin!' his two cousins yelled in triumph, and then doubled themselves up with laughing.

Dan felt utterly humiliated. He had done it again. In London he had two ways of talking English: one that he used at home; the other that he kept for school. Here at Danestone, he had come out with the wrong one.

'He's a wonderful cockney is Dan,' Nigel explained to the bewildered Henry.

Dan's rage with himself gave him courage. He had a ball in his left hand ready for his service; he had a racket in his right hand. And before him, on the other side of the net was Nigel's hateful, smirking face. He swung back the racket, took aim, and then slammed the ball as hard as he could straight at it.

'Look out,' yelled Henry.

'Good God!' shouted Simon in wonder. 'What ever are you up to?'

For instead of the ball going anywhere near

44

Nigel, it had shot off in a deadly spinning swoop, high over the privet hedge.

A second later came the crash of glass.

The four of them stood stock still, listening to the tinkle of falling splinters.

'It's the dining-room,' said Nigel.

'No. It's the study,' said Simon.

As Dan ran off round the side of the privet hedge to discover the worst, he met his grandfather striding out of the front door.

'What the devil!' the old man exploded.

'I'm sorry. It was me.'

'What ever were you at?'

'Trying to hit the ball at Nigel,' he blurted out.

Somehow his grandfather missed the point.

'But the court's a long way away,' he expostulated. 'And in any case you don't serve in this direction.'

'I know.'

'You must be a remarkably bad shot.'

'I am.'

And then, for no reason at all, his grandfather suddenly gave him one of his lop-sided smiles.

'I expect it's those glasses of yours,' he remarked.

Perhaps that was it, he thought dejectedly. Any other self-respecting boy would have got the ball plump in Nigel's face.

'Well, don't look so downhearted,' said his grandfather, clapping him on the shoulder. 'Accidents will happen. Accidents will happen. Now, while Rose sweeps up the glass on the study floor, you and I'll measure the size of the pane, and then you can run down to Mrs Mobbs. She'll get Mobbs to cut a new one and bring it up after lunch.'

By the time that Dan at last got back to the tennis court, he found Henry on his own, practising hand-stands under the cedar.

'Where are the others?' he asked.

'Gone off down the tow-path with their bathing things,' Henry replied, having swung himself the right way up. 'Their father's bringing the new speedboat up from Rushby.'

'And they left you?'

'No,' he grinned. 'I left them.'

'What do you mean?'

'I wanted to wait for you.'

Dan ran upstairs to fetch his own bathing kit and on the way out again looked in at the kitchen to tell his grandmother where they were going. It was a courtesy that was rewarded, for she offered him two hot currant buns from the batch she had just baked.

'They'll fill up the odd gap in you both,' she said. 'Besides, I expect you'll be late for lunch.'

Her kindness made him feel uncomfortable. Life here at Danestone could have been so easy and unfussed if only he hadn't spoilt it all – and this boy who was waiting for him could have been a friend if he hadn't told him such a ridiculous lie. He rejoined Henry, feeling wary and anxious.

'Buns?' Henry exclaimed joyfully, swinging himself down from a branch of the cedar. 'And all hot! How lovely.'

And Dan took in again the ugly, smiling face and the shabby clothes and wondered afresh how anyone so likeable could have come to have made friends with his horrible cousins.

'You don't really learn Chinese at your school, do you?' Henry asked between mouthfuls of bun.

Dan felt the colour rushing up into his face. It was out already – and he was undone.

'Of course not,' he muttered.

For one terrible moment Henry gave him a sharp, unfathomable look. Then his eyes suddenly filled with amusement.

'What a wonderful leg-pull!' he said, bursting out laughing. 'They believed every word . . . and so did I, till I saw you looking so desperate.'

'Desperate?'

'Why, if you'd really been learning Chinese, you'd have been so cock-a-hoop that you'd have looked smug.'

Well, thank God, thought Dan, that someone had seen through his lie.

He'd been quite right to make fools of them, Henry went on. They had behaved rottenly – all three of them. And they deserved it.

Dan blinked at him in astonishment. This was quite a new turn to affairs. Besides, he could not understand the boy's lack of contempt. Didn't it mean anything at Granthams when one was caught telling fibs?

And he suddenly felt so relieved and happy that he was safely out of this one particular mess that he wanted to shout. Jump ten feet high. Sail up to

Mars in a balloon. Instead, he made off towards the gate in the wall leading into the grassy lane, shouting back over his shoulder:

'Come on. I'll show you the marshes and the river.'

'I can't swim, you know,' said Henry catching up with him.

'I know. We'll muck about on the bank instead.'

He had forgotten about the maltings.

As they passed the old, familiar, rotting rowing-boat tipped over on its side and almost hidden in the nettles and rounded the corner on to the tow-path, there they were on the far side of the dike, lying in wait for him, every low, barred window seeming to stare at them with hostile eye. Dan wanted to hurry past for he was sure that the fierce boy must be watching them from behind a grating; but Henry stopped on the path exactly opposite the open door to point out the perfect reflections of the warm brick walls in the water. There was not a ripple anywhere in the dike. Nothing stirred. The silence of the place was daunting.

'Ever been in there?' he asked quietly. 'It looks spooky.'

'No,' Dan shouted. 'No. No. We mustn't go near it. It's out of bounds.'

His voice reverberated all over the marsh – and he fled.

'What's the matter?' Henry called out as he padded after him. 'Why are you shouting?'

Dan stopped out of earshot of the maltings and

tried to gather his wits together. It was just that they were crazy and tumbledown, he explained, and that his grandfather had made him promise not to go into them.

'He says they ought to have been boarded up years ago.'

Henry still looked puzzled; but he let it pass. And the two walked on together under the huge bowl of the sky, stopping every now and then to snatch handfuls of dead reed stems and throw them into the water and watch them float over the heads of the glancing minnows. They were drawn to each other in this first hour of their friendship yet both still felt wary and kept himself on guard. Dan was thinking: 'How can this boy possibly like my cousins? There must be something wrong with him that I haven't yet discovered.' And Henry was thinking: 'What on earth's the matter with those maltings to make him screech like an underground train?'

They had come now to Dan's uncle's new boathouse, built slap across the towpath, so that people walking along the dike had to plunge into the reeds at the back of the building before regaining the path on the far side.

'Just the blasted selfish thing he *would* do,' Nick had burst out last summer when he had first seen it.

It was his own piece of land, Dan had replied. And besides, where else could he have built it?

'Down by the river, of course. Not here, on a public footpath.'

This morning in the hot sunshine the

boathouse with its freshly-creosoted plank walls and its neat reed thatch wore an almost contemptuous air of wealth and well-being, standing there surrounded by the tangled growth of willow-herb, hemp agrimony, and purple loosestrife. Even its arrogant smell of disinfectant seemed an affront to anyone who loved the marsh.

'I wonder what it's like inside,' said Henry, walking round to the back and rattling the door.

'They keep it locked,' said Dan. 'But we can look inside if you want to. I'll show you.'

He dumped his bathing kit on the bank and climbed carefully out over the water along the narrow bar at the bottom of the water-gate, pushing his fingers through the wire-netting and holding tight to stop himself from falling off into the dike.

'Come on. It's quite easy.'

'Is the water deep?'

'Not more than four feet.'

Henry hated water. The thought of drowning put him in a panic. But his commonsense came to the rescue of his fear. Four feet of water would only come up to his shoulders. He surely couldn't drown even if he did fall in.

'I'm coming,' he said.

They peered into the shadowy boat-house at the sailing-boat drawn up on the concrete hard and at the paddles and boat-hook ranged along the walls and then at the sails and mast – and a beautiful canoe – slung up on the rafters in the roof, all dappled with the light reflected up from the water below.

'Where's their old motor launch?' Dan wondered aloud.

'They've sold it to help pay for the speedboat,' Henry replied. 'It's cost thousands of pounds. No wonder they keep this place locked.'

Dan let out a horse laugh.

'Bet I can burgle it in a matter of minutes,' he said with a grin.

'How?'

'Guess.'

Henry looked above his head and saw that the doors of the water-gate reached right up to the tie-beam of the roof and then he looked below his feet and saw that the wire-netting reached far below the surface of the water.

'Give up,' he said.

'Well, get back on to the bank and I'll show you. Nick did it last year . . . and . . . and I'm sure I could do it again now.'

Once they were both back on the bank, Dan stripped off his clothes and hurriedly pulled on his bathing trunks. He felt suddenly conscious of his London whiteness standing up in the great green sea of the marsh and, glancing back the way they had come, saw the maltings looming not half a mile away. The pagoda chimney was like a watch-tower. The spying boy flitted through his mind.

'Take care of my glasses,' he said, handing them over.

Then he did a belly-flop into the quiet dike and trod water for a moment while he looked back at Henry, feeling excited and happy. He wanted to prove that he could be as clever as Nick and – after his idiocy at tennis – he wanted to show Henry that he was really quite competent once he was swimming.

'Watch,' he shouted.

He pinched his nose between the fingers of his left hand and suddenly disappeared beneath a clump of water-crowfoot. The surface of the water bubbled deeply as though convulsed by an earthquake, the water-gate shook, and then – to Henry's astonishment – Dan's head and shoulders appeared in the deep cut of water inside the boathouse.

'Good Lord!' exclaimed Henry, as a mud-streaked Dan clambered up the concrete ramp and on to the hard. 'How on earth did you do that?'

'There's just . . . just eighteen inches,' he spluttered, 'between the bottom of the wire and the bottom of the dike.'

Then he lent far out over the water-gate and began groping about for its stout bolt and, having undone it, padded back to the rear of the boathouse and unwound a thin wire cable from its cleat and, pulling on it, opened one of the doors of the water-gate slowly inwards. It was easy, he shouted triumphantly. The other one opened the same way. Then he pushed the door outward again with the boathook, slid home the bolt, pulled the cable taut, and slithered back under the wire into the dike.

'That's how Nick got the launch out last year,' he explained proudly as he stood once more on the bank beside his friend.

'You mean he actually took it out of the boat-house?'

'Yes, he started up the engine and we went chugging up to Barlingham Lock and back.'

Henry let out a long, low whistle of admiration.

'And your Uncle George never knew?'

'No,' Dan grinned. 'They were all off sailing at Rushby Regatta.'

'Goodness!' Henry exclaimed. 'I'd never have had the courage. Your uncle's got the devil of a temper.'

'I know.'

Dan grinned even more widely. He loved to boast about Nick. And here, at last, was someone to whom he could talk about his brother.

Yet even as he rejoiced, he felt a check, for he saw that Henry's squashed nose was wrinkling up in disgust.

'Ugh!' he sniffed. 'And it smells, too!'

Dan, following his gaze, looked down at himself and saw that he was covered in mud. He sighed with relief. It was nothing, he said. It was only the bottom of the dike. He'd go in again and get it off. And he belly-flopped into the water once more and began swimming gently downstream towards the river.

'You'll only get yourself filthy again getting out,' Henry called after him.

'No, I shan't,' he yelled back, turning himself over to look at his friend. 'There's sand and gravel on the river bank at Danestone Beach. If you'll bring my glasses and clothes, I'll come ashore there. It's only about a hundred yards.'

Then, for a whole blissful minute, he gave himself up to floating like a log and to realizing how happy he was to be lying flat under the great, smiling sky, with the rat-holes in the banks gliding upstream on either side, and with Henry to talk to at his journey's end.

3

The Great Boy-Hunt Begins

EIGHTY miles to the west, Trevor Fincher of 14 Beech Tree Crescent, Cambridge woke slowly on that bright August morning and lay gazing up at the patterns on the ceiling made by the sunlight streaming through his bedroom curtains. He felt lazily content. He had worked hard all week. Very hard. And he deserved his Saturday lie-in. Then, thinking of the delights of the day that lay ahead of him, he peered at his watch, let out a yell, and hurled himself out of bed.

'Ma,' he shouted down the stairs. 'It's past eleven. Why the hell didn't you wake me up?'

''Cos you didn't ask me,' came the shrill reply from the kitchen. 'That's why.'

He pulled on his clothes in a terrible hurry. Then he went along to the bathroom and slicked his face and hair with water. He was panic-stricken. There was no time to shave. The gang was to meet up outside the American Cemetery in less than half an hour – and he was sure the others wouldn't wait. Why should they? He was new to them. This was to be his very first spin. He grabbed up his black leather jacket and the helmet with the cross-bones newly painted across the front and clumped angrily down towards the smell of burnt toast.

'I'll never make it,' he flung at his mother as she poured him a cup of stewed tea.

'You can go after them, can't you?'

'Yes,' he replied sullenly.

But it was not the same thing. Not at all the same thing. The Cambridge Crossbones were to rendezvous with the Watton Werewolves at the great roundabout at Barton Mills, and one of the chief joys of the day was to be hurtling down the Cambridge and Newmarket by-pass and out on to the A11 in a screaming phalanx of motor bikes, frightening the living daylight out of timid people in their Minis. To come limping six miles behind the gang on his beautiful new 250cc Suzuki was a miserable way to begin.

'Drink up your tea then,' his mother said. 'And be off with you. You can eat the toast as you go along.'

Trevor slurped down the cold tea, wiped his mouth with the back of his hand, put on his jacket and helmet, and strode out of the house, trying to make his eyes go slit like the spacemen in 'Star Trek'.

A moment later he was back again, white-faced and appalled.

'It's gone,' he gasped.

'What's gone?' snapped his mother, interrupted once again in reading her horoscope.

'The Suzuki.'

'The Suzuki?' she exclaimed, jumping up and running out to survey the empty front garden. 'Didn't you lock it up?'

'I . . . I thought I did.'

He looked stupid with shock.

'Well, you thought wrong,' she replied bitterly. 'That's for sure.'

He stood beside her staring at her striped petunias, stunned by the magnitude of his loss.

'What do I do?' he whispered.

'Go round to your precious Terry,' she replied tartly. 'And see if he's been up to his "borrowing" again. And if Terry hasn't got it, you'll have to go to the police.'

As she watched him trailing down the Crescent towards his friend, she felt stabbed with anguish for him. He hadn't yet realised the half of his misfortune. Then he turned and came back to her.

'Betts'll let me cancel the payments, won't they?' he asked. 'Now that I haven't got the bike?'

God in heaven! she thought. What *do* they teach them in the schools?

'They're a finance house,' she answered him. 'Not the Salvation Army.'

'What do you mean?' he gasped.

The Suzuki cost £850, she explained patiently as though to a child. He'd paid £130 down. But there was still the rest to pay off at £35 a month.

'And I'll have to go on paying?' he almost screamed.

She nodded.

'For three whole bloody years?'

'Cheer up,' she replied, with a total lack of conviction. 'The police may recover it. They sometimes do.'

Meanwhile back in the Danestone maltings, Trevor's beautiful Suzuki stood propped inside the furnace-house covered with greasy and rat-gnawed coal sacks, while Kevin Britton, who had put it there, sat huddled on the upper floor of the maltings desperately fighting off sleep. All the time that Dan had been having breakfast and later sitting up in the cedar tree contemplating life, he had been in a fever of fear that the child had told all to his grandfather. He had run from one window to another to peer out, determined never again to be taken by surprise; and it was only when he had heard the rhythmic 'ping ping' of tennis balls against rackets that he had allowed himself to relax. Simon and Nigel, talking as they walked down to the river, had woken him up with a start; and later he had watched Dan and Henry come out from the lane and stand exactly opposite him across the dike.

'I'm done for,' he had thought in panic. 'The kid hasn't told his grandfather but he'll tell this boy.'

Then from Dan's warning shout he realised that the child – unbelievably – was keeping their pact. The two boys walked on. Kevin, with the sweat running down his face, had peered after them through the barred window and wondered what the hell Dan was up to fooling about by the boat-house.

But he was too tired – too tired – to think any more. He slumped down by the plastic bag of bread and chicken stew, gave them a poke, and found that they had thawed out.

Perhaps eating something might help him stay awake.

Dan stopped gazing up at the blue August sky and rolled over and swam down the dyke into the wider waters of the River Waveney. Through a blur he saw Henry sitting on Danestone beach waiting for him.

'Where are the others?' he shouted. 'I thought Uncle George would be here with the speedboat.'

'Water-skiing most like,' Henry shouted back.

'*Water-skiing?*' he exclaimed in astonishment as he began wading ashore. 'You mean Simon and Nigel have actually learnt how to *water-ski?*'

They were learning, Henry explained. Last week they had had three lessons with an instructor down on Oulton Broad.

'That's what they want the speedboat for – so that your uncle can go whizzing them up and down the river up here.'

'Gosh! Lucky things!'

Dan was not given to envy. But this was too much for him. He had seen people water-skiing on television and had thought it a most beautiful and miraculous thing to go skimming over the surface of the water as graceful and as weightless as a flying bird. He wished that they'd let *him* have a go. But he knew that they wouldn't. There'd always be some excuse. He'd be too clumsy or too short-sighted or else there wouldn't be time. Asking Henry for his glasses and his towel, he began rubbing himself dry far too hard, trying to put his jealousy out of his mind. But the thought of his cousins water-skiing was like a huge stone thrown into a small pond. It sent waves of disgust lashing out in every direction. Damn Uncle George's wealth! Damn all the things it gave them that he and Nick had never had! And – worst of all – he thought, damn the whole family for thinking that they were so much better than anyone else!

'I'd stop if I were you,' said Henry mildly. 'You're rubbing yourself sore.'

He looked down to find his new friend smiling up at him and felt strangely rebuked. Henry was so ugly and so shabby – and he couldn't even swim – yet he didn't seem to mind. He must have some secret greatness, he thought, that no one knew about except himself – like the beggar in the fairy-story who was really a prince in disguise. He looked down at Henry's boxer's nose, the patched shirt, and the toe coming through the sneaker and found this such a happy idea that as he smiled back he found somehow that his cousins' grandness didn't matter quite so much. They could keep their damned speedboat and their skis and their posh school and all the other show-off trappings of Uncle George's fat money-bags. He'd just not bother to care any more.

Besides, as he stood there on the beach, naked now except for his glasses, he saw that this was too glorious a day to waste on his cousins. The sunlight was pouring down on the river where a slight breeze blowing upstream against the ebb tide had ruffled up millions of ripples. Each now was a flashing gold-and-silver fish, darting, leaping, diving – always on the move. He loved the river when it was like this. He loved everything about it: the feathery tops to the reeds on the far shore; the smell of marsh mint and meadowsweet and wet mud; the plop of fish; even the flies. And he liked the vastness of its valley. Far away to the east he could see Rushby church tower sticking up on the horizon like a man's thumb; and when he turned round and gazed back along the way they had come he saw Danestone village stretched out in a thin, broken line between the dead elms and the wheatfields rising towards Thursby and the flat marsh-grazing close at hand. Then he saw the menacing pagoda-roofed chimney of the maltings – and he quickly ducked down behind the rampart of willow-herb to be out of sight. He tugged on his clothes again, longing to be left unbothered for once.

It was quiet and shut-in on the beach. It was safe. They both must have felt that they were at last on their own, for they sat on for a little in a comfortable silence – as only friends can – gazing at the river.

'You must miss him,' Henry said after a while.

'Nick?'

'It must be awful for you being down here on your own. . . .'

Dan turned away his face. There was nothing he could say.

'I'd've loved to have met him. I've heard so much about him. . . .

Dan scowled. He wondered what his cousins had said.

'He must have been frightfully bright. Your Aunt Philippa says he answered every question put to him in 'Top of the Form'. . . .

Dan relaxed a little.

'And he wasn't a bit of a prig or a swot . . . or . . . or one of those ghastly grown-ups' darlings.'

No, Dan agreed. Nick had certainly not been that.

'In fact,' laughed Henry, 'he was absolutely wild.'

Hadn't he been suspended once for flooding the girls' needlework-room at the Comprehensive? Hadn't he, when he was a choir-boy, slipped up into the pulpit and laced the vicar's glass of water with a slug of gin?

Dan nodded – and then waited. It would not be too bad if Nick's crimes stopped there.

'And didn't he once try running away to sea? Making for Rio, so your uncle said.'

'He was very young,' said Dan by way of excuse.

Henry shot him a puzzled look. He misunderstood.

'But it was a splendid thing to do at any age.'

Dan kept his brother's secret. Nick had always hated anything inefficient. By some childish error he had chosen the wrong vessel and had been picked up ignominiously in the hold of a cargo-boat making for Rotterdam.

There was a silence then in which each followed his own thoughts. Henry was seeing in his mind's eye a swashbuckling latter-day Sir Walter Raleigh or Sir Francis Drake. Dan was thanking his stars that Nick had got off so lightly.

But perhaps, he concluded, his cousins hadn't really known any more. Perhaps his parents and his grandparents had kept Nick's other misdemeanours a secret.

'It seems dreadful,' sighed Henry, 'that someone with so much guts should have been killed in a stupid accident.'

Dan clutched at a handful of sand and then – as Henry said no more – stopped holding his breath and released the grains to trickle free through his fingers.

Soon after this they heard the distant, low scream of the speedboat.

'They're coming,' shouted Dan, eagerly jumping to his feet and looking upstream.

Gone was his envy. Gone was his well-intentioned contempt.

The scream of the speed-boat had now risen to a roar.

'There they are,' shouted Henry.

They could see Simon's head over the top of the reeds as he skied towards them down the next reach. They could hear his father's voice barking out instruction.

'Good. Good. You're doing well,' he bellowed over the roar of the engine. 'Now remember the landing drill. When I turn away from the beach, swing in towards it and let go the rope. And glide. *Glide*.'

The prow of a gleaming red speedboat came into view round the bend and, a moment later, the speedboat, the entire ploughed river, and Simon clad all in black rubber like a Martian skimming along the furrow, came hurtling towards them. It was a breath-taking sight. There was a boy – a boy they actually knew – flying over the top of the water. And behind him, the reed beds on either side were tossing up and down like a vast crowd running along a towpath to keep up with the race. . . .

'If you're going too fast, sit down in the water,' bawled Uncle George, heading the boat straight at the two of them standing there on the little beach.

Dan grabbed Henry. Behind them was the willow-herb and a six-foot bank of stinging nettles.

'Get back as far as you can,' he shouted, as the speedboat swerved away and Simon lunged sideways and then let go the rope.

'Good God,' gasped Henry, fleeing from the narrow shelf of sand.

Simon in his gleaming wet-suit was whizzing

straight at them like something released from a catapult.

'Sit down in the water,' yelled his father.

'Get out of the way,' shrieked Simon.

A second later he shot right over the narrow spit of sand and knocked them both down. He landed on top of them in a smother of sharp-edged skis, red-hot nettles, and angry abuse. And, before they could sort themselves out, the river caught up with them. The sweeping wash from the speedboat rolled up over the strand and drenched them all.

Henry had let out a yelp and was now rubbing his shin. Dan could see him through his smashed glasses biting his lip. Blood was oozing through a new gash in his patched jeans.

'You great oaf,' he shouted at his cousin as he struggled to his feet. 'Just look what you've done!'

'Why the hell did you two just stand there?' Simon hurled back.

'We didn't.'

But it was Uncle George who had the last word. He had turned the speedboat full circle and was now bellowing his displeasure from close at hand.

'You damned fool, Simon,' he bawled. 'You might have snapped your skis. Why didn't you sit down in the water as I told you?'

The same red-faced old turkey-cock, thought Dan. And not a word about Henry's bashed leg.

The three of them had sorted themselves out by now and were standing upright on the beach, bruised, stung, angry, and sopping wet.

'Golly, you do look funny,' laughed Nigel.

He was sitting in his black wet-suit beside his father, looking just like a fat slug.

'Hallo, Dan,' said Uncle George in a milder voice. 'Glad to see you. Sorry we've drenched you both. But it'll soon dry.'

Then turning to Nigel, he barked:

'Well, hurry up. It's your turn again now. Let's see if you can't make a better job of it this time.'

The slug's smile died in his face.

'Crouch down in the water and then lean forward till your chest touches your knees,' said Simon as he took his brother's place in the boat.

Dan, looking down at Henry's bare feet, saw that one of them was becoming streaked with little rivulets of blood. Henry, frowning, followed his gaze.

'It's only a graze,' he muttered, and then added, smiling wryly. 'It's my jeans that I'm worrying about. I think that's finished them.'

'And then as we gather speed,' Simon shouted to his brother 'and you begin planing along the surface, pull yourself upright.'

'I *know*,' burst out the exasperated Nigel.

'But you don't *do* it,' laughed Simon.

'I expect my grandmother'll be able to do something about them,' Dan told Henry. 'She usually can.'

Once, twice, three times the unhappy Nigel tried to get himself launched on his skis, but each time that he stood upright the river suddenly opened its mouth and swallowed him up. By common consent, Dan and Henry could bear it no longer. They began trailing away home along the tow-path in their sopping clothes pursued by the angry sounds of the lesson they were leaving behind.

'You're *still* doing it too jerkily,' shouted Simon.

'I can't *do* it,' wailed Nigel.

'Yes, you *can*,' thundered Dan's Uncle George. 'Try again.'

Dan grinned at Henry.

'We've not got their beastly money,' he blurted out. 'But I bet we've both of us got much nicer fathers.'

Henry did not respond at once. His leg must be giving him hell, Dan thought.

Then his friend stooped down and picked up a clod of clay and threw it expertly at a water-lily leaf in the dyke.

'I've got a wonderful Mum,' he said cheerfully. 'A really wonderful Mum.'

Kevin Britton's attack on the police constable and his subsequent escape in the stolen Allegro had been radioed to every police headquarters in the country soon after midnight. A warning had been added to the message: 'The boy's dangerous. He's armed.' Eleven and a half hours later, the Cambridge police, alerted by the theft of Trevor Fincher's Suzuki, put two and two together and swooped on the northern suburbs of the City – and at midday, they came upon the white Allegro. In a matter of minutes they were on to the incident room set up at Wellingborough to deal with the crime.

'We've got your Higham Ferrers stolen Allegro,' announced Inspector English with understandable satisfaction.

'Be damned you have,' came the crusty reply. 'You sure?'

'Same registration number – and a squashed Mars Bar under the front seat. Want any more?'

'That's it. Good for you. We'll be over. Sorry for the flak. We've had "positive" sightings coming in all morning. Durham, Leicester, Walton le Willows – and now Knotty Green.'

'Christ! Where's that?'

'Just outside Beaconsfield. Any sign of the boy?'

'No. But we think he got away on a 250cc Suzuki,' replied the inspector, and he gave the registration number.

'The little bastard.'

'Full tank. T registration. Those borstal lads always choose themselves winners.' Then, belatedly, the Cambridge inspector remembered the injured policeman. 'How's your P.C. Jeffers.'

'Off duty with a kick in the groin.'

'Poor devil. No worse?'

'Bad enough when you're young and been made to look a fool.'

Then they got back to business. Their Cambridge Scene-of-Crime chap was on the job now, said Inspector English. There were plenty of fingerprints coming up.

'Any incidents in your patch involving Suzukis?' asked the detective inspector at Wellingborough.

'I'll check. But not that I know of.'

'Then we'll have to radio all stations again. Many thanks. We'll keep you informed.'

Half an hour later, the motor-cycle incidents came pouring in. A young man killed on the M4 at junction 8/9; neither body nor make of machine yet identified. Accidents involving Suzukis at Bicester, Canterbury, Clifton, and Weymouth. A motor cycle seen by a G.P. out attending a heart attack roaring through the village of Brockdish at two in the morning. Two Suzukis stolen in the night: one in Lincoln; one in Freshwater, Isle of Wight.

'Take your pick, sir,' said the young officer, presenting his superior with the report.

'Brockdish.'

'Where's Brockdish, sir?'

'Norfolk/Suffolk border. A143. Good restaurant. That's my bet. Alert Norwich, Bury St Edmunds, Lowestoft, and Ipswich. Give registration number of the Suzuki and full description of Kevin Britton. Tell them trouble's headed their way. And tell them also that we're warning the public on radio and television not to tackle him themselves. He's dangerous. He's got that gun. With luck we'll get a photograph of him out in time for the Sunday papers.'

4
Sunday

Nᴏᴛ one of them at The Old House, Danestone listened to the news on that Saturday afternoon and evening. The reason was simple. Dan had long ago stopped bothering to attend to the daily catalogue of earthquakes, famine, bombings, strikes, redundancies, and lay-offs which so consistently afflicted the adult world. The disasters were too remote and too repetitive. He had closed his mind to them years ago – as one learns to close one's mind to a long November drizzle. His grandmother, on the other hand, was – quite simply – too busy. There were meals to be cooked. Anguished though she might be by the starving nations of the world, she had always devoted her Augusts to the feeding of her grandsons. Now that, tragically, there was only one of them, her task had become even more compulsive. She cooked for Dan as though she were cooking for the five thousand. Dan's grandfather, by contrast, had all the time in the world and the liveliest of interests in its goings-on. At ten minutes to the hour he pulled out his father's old hunter, gave it a tap, and then padded off to his study and turned on the radio. By the end of the weather forecast he was fast asleep. He was seventy-two. It was one of the odder penalties of growing old.

The three of them, therefore, set off to church on that hot Sunday morning unaware of the latest outrage of violent youth, each wrapped in silent thought. Colonel Henchman's meditations were biblical rather than religious. They ran on the lesson that he was about to read from the Book of Daniel. It was the chapter describing King Nebuchadnezzar's command that all his people should bow down and worship his golden image whenever they heard the sound of the 'Cornet, flute, harp, sackbut, psaltery, dulcimer, and all kinds of musick'. Three times he had to repeat the names of this outlandish Babylonian orchestra – and three times he would want to laugh, as he had laughed as a boy. And what, for Pete's sake, had Nebuchadnezzar and the blare of his pagan band got to do with quiet, hard-working Danestone, now girding itself for the last of the harvest? He did not know. There was so much that he did not know. He sighed. The older he grew the more puzzled and uncertain of things he was becoming. Take this other Daniel, for example, this bespectacled, well-mannered grandson walking at his side. What was he to make of the boy? He was so quiet, so shut up inside himself, so unlike the open, friendly child of last summer, that he felt faced by a stranger. How could he get through to him again? All the bridges seemed to have been blown up. Then glancing down, he saw that Dan was smiling. 'Well, thank God for that,' he

71

thought. 'Perhaps he's found a button to put in the offertory bag.'

Mrs Henchman's musings were more practical and down-to-earth. She wondered whether Mrs Thurgar had remembered to fill up the water in the altar vases. Even church flowers were apt to wilt in this August heat. And then her mind went back to Henry. She had worried about him all night. Yesterday, when the two boys had returned from the river dripping with mud and water, she had ordered them both into the bath, while she threw their clothes into the washing-machine. Then, looking out a jumble T-shirt, vest, and socks collected for the Women's Institute Fair and a patched pair of jeans that Nick had kept at Danestone especially for climbing trees, she had put sticking plaster on the boy's shin and sent them both down to lunch. Later, a closer inspection of Henry's pants and vest hanging on the washing-line had filled her with dismay. They were so patched and cobbled together that they were fit for nothing but the dustbin. 'Poor boy! Poor boy!' she thought in puzzled distress. 'If he were not so clearly calm and happy, I'd say he was dreadfully neglected.' What was such a poverty-stricken boy doing at Granthams, she wondered, and how had he come to make friends with her two spoilt, over-indulged grandsons at The Grange? Then she, too, glanced at Dan and saw him smiling to himself. She looked away quickly, swept with love for the child, but fearing to intrude. She had been right. As she climbed the steep steps up into Danestone churchyard, she felt quietly pleased with herself. Dan had wanted a friend. She had found him Henry.

Dan, however, walking silently between them, was smiling for quite a different reason. A great burden had been lifted from his shoulders and he felt as innocent again and as light and carefree as the thistledown now taking wing all over the unweeded churchyard. He had woken at midnight in the summer-house and looked up at the stars and had suddenly realised with unbounded relief that the maltings must now be empty. The fierce boy had left Danestone – as he had promised to do; he had walked out of his life. He, Dan, could forget all about him, rid himself for ever of the boy's mysterious troubles and of his own uncomfortable feelings of guilt. With Henry as a companion, he could begin his holiday here all over again.

As they passed the group of mouldering Henchman tombs, Dan glanced happily across the seeding churchyard and caught the eye of Jim Foulger, who was heading along the path that led to the choirboys' door. To his surprise Jim gave him the most horrible scowl.

What on earth was the matter?

He and Henry had met Jim only yesterday afternoon on the Rushby quay. Aunt Philippa had driven them both over to pick up Uncle George and the cousins, who were sailing their boat down from Danestone to be ready for the first race in the Rushby Regatta on Monday morning. And, upon Aunt Philippa leaving them to go shopping up the town, they had wandered about the meadow

73

behind the quay where the gypsies were busy setting up their annual fair. Jim had come sidling up to them with his sleepy grin as they had stood watching the roundabout going up.

'Yew down here for long?' he had asked Dan.

'A month.'

'Yew'll come fishin' agin up at t'lock?'

'Yes . . . Yes . . . I'd like that. I'd like it very much.'

Dan had felt himself blush with pleasure at the boy's kindness, for last summer Jim had been Nick's friend rather than his.

All this time Jim had been giving Henry the slow once-over. He must have approved of the bright eyes and the crooked nose and the jumble T-shirt and Nick's old jeans for he had promptly included him too in the invitation.

'Yew comin' along with him?'

'I'd like to.'

'I'll be seein' yew then,' he had grinned.

And he had sloped off between the coloured booths.

Why now was Jim giving him such a furious and hating look? What had he done?

The three of them had now entered the church and a minute later they were in the Henchman pew and kneeling on the Mothers Union hassocks. Dan, opening his fingers as he prayed, saw Henry and the Heseltines entering the pew immediately in front of them. And his mind flew from Jim and his odd behaviour to the even odder things he had learnt about Henry.

Yesterday afternoon, when his cousins had

finished stowing the gear of the sailing boat, they had joined Henry and himself on the fairground. In the course of things the four of them had divided up. Nigel and Henry had stayed behind to have free shies at the coconuts while he and Simon had wandered on.

'Since you're getting so friendly with Henry,' Simon had said, 'there's something you ought to know about him.'

'Ought I?'

'His father's run away with a night-club queen.'

Dan was hazy about night-clubs and had certainly never suspected that they had queens. But he saw Henry's plight.

'You mean he's left his mother for good?'

'Of course I do. What else could I mean?'

It was pathetic really, Simon had gone on. Henry's mother was working her guts out to pay for his fees at school. And since she worked so hard, all day and every day and often right through the holidays, Henry was left on his own when he went home.

For Dan the light was at last beginning to dawn.

'So *that*'s why he's staying with you?' he blurted out.

'That's it. The parents in our House take it in turns. He's very nice, you know. Nobody minds. But it's all no good.'

'What's no good?'

'Father says that even if she manages to scrape up enough money for Granthams, she'll never be able to afford to send him to Winchester or Marlborough or the kind of schools that the rest of us are going on to. It's impossible, he says, on what a librarian earns.'

Dan got up from the hassock, sat back on the pew seat, and stared at the nape of Henry's neck, liking his new friend more and more and wondering afresh how anyone could have so many troubles and remain so cheerful.

By this time the choir had processed into the chancel and the congregation was rising to its feet.

'"When the wicked man"' declared Mr Micklethwaite in resounding tones, '"turneth away from his wickedness that he hath committed and doeth that which is lawful and right, he shall save his soul alive."'

Dan was fast falling into his usual Sunday dream when the church suddenly echoed to a dreadfully rude expletive. He blushed scarlet. The word had come from the front row of the choir. It had come from Jim.

'"Dearly beloved brethren,"' Mr Micklethwaite continued in a hurry.

And the congregation throughout that notorious morning service bellowed out the responses and bellowed out the hymns – as though bellowing were the only way to erase the dreadful word that had defiled its church.

That afternoon Henry and Dan, spinning along the dusty lanes on the cousins' bicycles, came upon Jim sitting on a gate. They stopped pedalling, swooped round, and came to a halt at his feet.

'What ever made you do that?' Dan asked. 'It shocked everybody out of their wits.'

Jim was still looking mutinous.

'That's what I meant to do,' he snarled.

'But *why*? What's happened?'

'The wicked turnin' from his wickedness and goin' to heaven . . . it's all crap,' he jeered. 'And it's time those mumbling old fools sittin' in the nave knew all about it.'

'Who's been getting at you?' asked Dan, remembering Jim's past.

'P'lice. Woke us up at half-past two, me Mum and me, wantin' to know where I'd been all night. Came right up to me bedroom and looked at me clothes.'

'But why?'

''Cos of that break-in at Mavers shop.'

'Mavers?'

'Over at Thursby. Where we buy our maggots.'

Dan remembered now. It was the Thursby village shop.

'But why *you*?' asked Henry.

''Cos two years back,' came the sullen reply. 'I took to knockin' off the Hall's pheasants with me catapult and sellin' 'em to the Rushby man. That's why.'

'Two years? But that's ages ago!'

'Like as I say,' Jim replied with a new spurt of anger. 'There's no forgiveness of sins . . . not here in Danestone.'

Every time someone nicked a bike or bashed up a telephone kiosk or pinched money out of the poor-box, he went on, the police were round trying to put the crime on him. He was sick of it. They'd even suspected him of stripping the lead off Wainstead church roof. It wasn't fair. He'd gone straight as a die since those pheasants – and it hadn't helped him a bit.

Henry and Dan agreed that it was monstrous. Police and magistrates and grown-ups in general ought to behave as they were told to behave in the Prayer Book.

'But what happened at the break-in?' asked Dan. 'Was much stolen?'

'Ma Mavers' week's takin's – so she says. Silly old bag kept them in a jar marked "Aniseed Balls". Everybody from t'other side of Wainstead to t'other side of Rushby knew that.'

But it wasn't a local job, Jim went on. He was sure of that. It was right out of the Waveney Valley class. It was far too professional. Pane of glass over the lock cut with something like a diamond and a gob of gum used to stop the glass from falling. And once inside, the thief hadn't bothered with anything save the money and two bottles of pop.

'Bottles of pop?' reiterated Dan, beginning to feel an odd fear creeping into his mind.

Suddenly Jim laughed.

'Well he didn't get far with them, he didn't.'

In the absence of a burglar alarm or a proper lock, he explained, Mrs Mavers was in the habit of leaving the trapdoor open down to her coal cellar. It was close to the door of the shop. The intruder had missed it on the way in but had fallen through to the Mavers' coal on the way out, smashing the two bottles of pop.

'Must've given him a real nasty shake-up,' he grinned. 'That's what the p'lice on the beat thought.'

'And that's why they wanted to see your clothes?' Henry asked.

'And to see if I'd got any bruises.'

'So you're in the clear?' asked Dan anxiously. 'They don't suspect you any more?'

'They'd better not – seein' as I didn't do it.'

He jumped down off the gate. Telling the tale of the break-in had somehow brought him back to cheerfulness.

'Have they chucked you out of the choir?' Dan asked.

Jim nodded.

''Bout time too,' he said. 'Me voice's been breakin' these last three months. I've been screeching like a crow.'

'Didn't anybody notice?'

'Nope. Nobody 'cept meself. We make such a bleedin' row up in that chancel, nobody'd know if we'd brought in a cock'rel.'

Behind Jim, standing there beside them on the grass verge, Dan saw the long stretch of the lane back to Danestone with its stark dead elms lined up like skeleton guards to protect Mr Fenton's forty-acre field. The farmer was out getting in the last of his wheat. The shimmer of the hot air above the roadway and the putter of the combine harvester and the green blackberries shrivelling in the hedgerow came to him almost unnoticed. But they were to stay in his mind for years – unimportant in themselves – yet a vivid reminder of Jim's returning friendship and of the extra-ordinary events which followed in those scorching August days.

'Be seein' yew then tomorrow mornin'?' Jim said as he turned to walk back to Danestone. 'At Barling'm Lock?'

'Yes, but why not call for us at my grandparents'?'

Jim stopped, turned round, and then shook his head.

'That's what you used to do last summer with Nick.'

Jim gave a wry, embarrassed smile.

'Don't think they'd care for me much, yer grandparents wouldn't, not after what I did in church.'

Dan let him go. He was right. His grandparents had been appalled.

'What ever got into the boy?' his grandmother had exclaimed at lunch.

'Quite simple, my dear,' his grandfather had replied. 'The devil.'

'But, Roland, you don't believe in the devil.'

'I'm not so sure, Madge. I'm not at all so sure. The older I grow the more of his works I see.'

Dan stood watching his friend loping home to his mother's cottage, quite unable to see horns sprouting out of Jim's head or his feet turning into cloven hoofs.

'Soon after nine, then,' he shouted after him.

'Let's go and have a look at that Thursby shop,' suggested Henry, as they got on their bikes again. 'The police and the detectives may still be there.'

'All right.'

Dan had so much to attend to that they rode on in silence while he tried to sort things out. He thought of Jim's unenviable lot in having to go on living in Danestone with that terrible word echoing and re-echoing round Danestone church. Nobody would ever forget it. It would dog him for years and years – perhaps for the rest of his life. And then he wondered if Jim had not been right: that no one was ever really forgiven for the things that he had done wrong. They went on hanging round his neck like that old man's albatross. Perhaps that was why the fierce boy was skulking in the maltings. He'd done something dreadful and no one was prepared to forgive him. Nobody would let him get back to the kind of person that he'd been before. And so he'd had to go on and on, perhaps even to breaking into the Thursby shop and stealing Mrs Mavers' takings. That was it. Once you'd begun you couldn't stop. Life must be arranged like that. And, with a sickening lurch, he thought of Nick taking Uncle John's new M.G. and driving it straight into that lorry. Well, they couldn't chase Nick any farther. He was dead.

'Yer too late,' shouted Tom Catchpole, as they rode out on to Thursby green. 'They've all gone home.'

Dan knew Tom from earlier summers. He was the son of the police constable at Wainstead Bottom. He was nine years old.

'Have they found any clues?' asked Henry, who'd just discovered Sherlock Holmes.

'A lot of fingerprints,' replied the policeman's son.

The S.O.C. man had been out from Rushby, he said, dressed in his long white coat, and he'd gone puffing his black dust stuff all over the place. But they hadn't sorted out yet which fingerprints belonged to Ma Mavers and her customers and which to the thief.

'There's nothing to see,' he shouted after them as they rode down the street. 'Yer too late. Yew should've been here this mornin'.'

But he was wrong. When they came to the shop, there *was* something to see.

Back in the incident room at Wellingborough, everyone was scratching his head. Not a single sighting of the missing boy had been reported in the last fourteen hours.

'He must be *somewhere*!' exclaimed the

Detective Inspector in exasperation. 'The little horror can't have ridden that Suzuki off the face of the earth.'

'Perhaps he's lying up with relations, sir,' suggested Detective Sergeant Lark. 'What about his parents?'

The Inspector shook his head gloomily. They'd taken themselves off to Plymouth, he said. And one didn't get to Plymouth by way of Brockdish, Norfolk.

'Plymouth? That's a long way from Northampton, sir.'

'I'd have gone farther if I'd had Kevin Britton for a son,' snapped the Inspector. 'I'd 've emigrated to Alaska.'

'What about his friends, sir? His old Borstal contacts?'

'I've thought of that. We're on to them now. So far, no luck.'

'How much money had he got on him, sir. Do we know?' asked W.P.C. Susan Feather.

'Only a few pence, I should think. That's all he got from the till at Higham Ferrers.'

'Well, sir . . . I've been thinking. He's got to *eat*.'

'To eat? Why so he has.'

'And . . . and, sir, if he's not getting food from friends, then he'll have to buy it . . . or . . . or steal it.'

'That's it! Good lass. Sergeant, radio all headquarters in the country immediately for details of break-ins at supermarkets, pubs, restaurants, cafés, village shops . . . anything you can think of . . . that have taken place in the last fourteen hours.'

Henry had particularly long eyesight. As they rode on towards Thursby village shop, he read the painted sign over the window: EMILY B. MAVERS: NEWSAGENT AND GENERAL STORE.

'That boy's right,' he said, looking over his shoulder at Dan dreaming along behind him. 'There's nothing to see. The place is all locked up. But there's a wonderful caption on the poster for your local Sunday paper.'

'What's it say?' asked Dan without interest.

'It says THE GREAT BOY HUNT. Sounds as though girls round here must be short of boys.'

'The Great Boy Hunt?' repeated Dan, suddenly roused and filled with unease.

It was like waking and hearing the sound of the alarm clock before it had actually gone off.

When they came to the shop, it was certainly deserted and the blinds were down in the front rooms of the cottage alongside, as though – disgusted by the night's doings – Ma Mavers and her husband had taken themselves out for the day. They had left something behind them, however; and this something drew Dan like a magnet. It was a small pile of the few remaining copies of the 'East Anglian Sunday News' left weighted down on an upturned orange-box by a brick and a tin for the money.

Dan got off his cousin's bike, leant it against the shop window, and went over and peered at what he could see of the paper's front page.

Then he let out a yelp.

The fierce boy had got himself out of the maltings and was there on the orange-box in black and white, staring up at him in angry defiance.

'What's the matter?' exclaimed Henry.

Dan looked dreadful – as though he'd suddenly come face to face with Dracula.

At that moment a car, which had been cruising slowly down the road behind them, stopped outside the shop, and a familiar voice called out:

'Is there a copy left for both of us, Dan?'

It was Mr Micklethwaite.

Kevin Britton's newspaper face seemed to have turned Dan into stone.

'Yes, sir,' replied Henry. 'I think there's three left. Shall I get you one?'

'Many thanks. Here's ten pence for the box.'

And away went the Vicar for the afternoon service at Wainstead Bottom.

'Are you all right?' asked Henry anxiously. 'You look dreadful.'

''ve you got any money on you?' was all Dan said. 'Can you buy me a copy?'

'What, *that* rag?'

'I want it.'

Dan sounded desperate.

Henry fumbled about in all his pockets and finally came up with a tenpenny piece stuck to a toffee.

'Here you are. What on earth do you want the paper for?'

'Tell you later. Not now,' Dan muttered, stuffing the paper in his pocket and walking shakily back to the two bicycles.

He headed for the loneliest, most forgotten place he knew: the tumbledown quay at Wainstead Staithe. Nick and he had discovered it last summer and had returned to it again and again. He pedalled furiously over the old level-crossing and down the rutted cart-track, past the disused brick kiln, and out over the naked marsh, Nigel's bicycle rearing beneath him like a frightened horse as it careered over the hoof-pocked turf.

'Goodness, whatever's the matter with him,' wondered the bewildered Henry, bumping crazily along behind him.

At the water's edge, Dan flung down the bicycle, sat down on the quay, and grabbed the newspaper out of his pocket. Henry sat down beside him and waited.

'Gosh!' exclaimed Dan in horror. 'He's shot at a policeman!'

'Who has?'

'This boy: Kevin Britton,' he replied, pointing to the picture in the paper.

Henry peered over his shoulder at the smouldering eyes and the fierce set of the jaw.

'That's awful,' he said. 'But what's it got to do with you?'

'He was in the maltings – *our* maltings all yesterday.'

'In that spooky place . . . by the dike?'

Dan nodded.

'He was there while we walked past on the way to the river?'

Dan nodded again. He was still deep in the account of the boy given in the paper.

'They're hunting for him all over the country,' he said at last. 'He's dangerous. He's got a gun.'

Henry grabbed the newspaper and read the article for himself.

'Police throughout the country are looking for an escaped Borstal boy, Kevin Britton, aged 16; height 5 foot 10 inches, last seen wearing a grey shirt, navy blue anorak and blue jeans. He has blue eyes and light brown hair. This boy is wanted in connection with a series of robberies and for attacking a policeman in resisting arrest. He is believed to be riding a Suzuki 250cc, registration number XYF 596T and to be somewhere in the Norfolk/Suffolk area. Members of the public who can give any information about this boy are asked to contact their local police immediately or phone Wellingborough 76011. They are warned not to approach the boy themselves. HE IS DANGEROUS. HE CARRIES A GUN.'

'How do you know he was in the maltings?' Henry asked, looking up from the paper.

Dan told his sorry tale.

'But why didn't you tell your grandfather straight away?'

'Why should I? I thought he'd had a row with someone . . . and just run away. It's . . . it's no crime just to run away.'

Dan felt shifty – and looked it.

'A boy with a gun?'

'I didn't see he had a gun. He . . . he must've got rid of it.'

'I don't know. It sounds pretty queer to me. Even without a gun, behaving so oddly and looking like that picture . . . you must've guessed that he'd done something dreadful.'

'I didn't really,' said Dan lamely. 'Besides, I . . . I sort of promised.'

And he explained about his grandfather forbidding him to go into the maltings and about his getting the boy food and a bottle of milk. Couldn't Henry see that they'd made a kind of pact? One couldn't go back on a pact.

'Sounds a pretty one-sided one to me,' Henry replied drily. 'What did he promise you in return?'

'That he'd be out of the maltings by this morning.'

'Was he?'

'Of course. Why shouldn't he be? No one would want to stay there all night if he could help it . . . not with all those rat droppings. Besides, I bet it was he who broke into Ma Mavers'.'

'And then buzzed off on that motor bike?'

'That's it,' replied Dan staring at the glinting water of the Waveney.

Henry looked at him sideways.

'What are you going to do now?'

Dan had dreaded this question.

What *was* he going to do?

He had been afraid of this Kevin Britton towering over him at the top of the ladder. He was now greatly shocked at hearing what he had done to the policeman. But the boy's terror . . . his terror of being caught . . . and the look on his face when he had brought him the food had somehow caught him in a vice. Kevin Britton was a thief and a bully, yet for some reason that he could not understand, Dan kept thinking of Nick – and of Jim shouting out his frightful word in church – and of everyone from Cain to the Ancient Mariner who had been caught up in the dreadful things they had done.

'It's no point doing anything, is it?' he stalled. 'He's miles away by now.'

'Are you saying that because you're afraid of your grandfather?'

Dan flushed with anger.

'Of course not.'

Is that what Henry really thought?

'I think it's much better to tell him,' Henry went on. 'And leave him to decide whether you ought to tell the police.'

'I don't,' Dan snapped.

He knew exactly what his grandfather would do. He had been a magistrate for years and years . . . until he'd become too old.

'How's it going to help anyone to know that he was in the maltings on Friday night?' he asked angrily.

'It might.'

Blast Henry, he thought.

'I suppose *you'll* tell him, if I don't,' he blurted out, meaning to hurt.

It was Henry's turn to flush.

'It's your secret. Not mine.'

'So you won't tell?'

'No.'

Dan stared out over the river at the Norfolk bank feeling miserably unhappy. Afraid of his grandfather? He longed for Henry to like him and respect him. Yet it was clear that he thought him a coward: that he was too afraid to own up that he'd been in the maltings and had stolen food for the boy. Was it true? *Was* he afraid? As the two of them sat on in silence, kicking their feet against the rotten quay, he tried to think honestly about himself and – in so doing – came upon something hardly more comforting than being thought a coward. It was that he had always been dull and ordinary and well-behaved, while Nick – for all his wildness – had always made people laugh. Nick had done everything with style. He, himself, had always fumbled. He had fumbled again about this boy in the maltings. And grown-ups wouldn't forgive fumblers. They wouldn't forgive someone who had always been 'good old Dan' for doing something utterly foolish.

'Of course you're right,' Henry dropped into the silence. 'He must be miles away by now . . . but . . .'

Dan looked up into his kind but puzzled face.

'. . . but what about Jim?'

'Jim?'

'His fingerprints may be in the shop . . . if he buys his maggots there.'

'Yes, but won't Kevin Britton's be there too?'

'Borstal may have taught him to wear gloves.'

Henry's superior knowledge made Dan feel very uneasy.

'They'd surely not accuse Jim of something he didn't do?'

'I don't know. It's clear the police don't like him. And I don't think Danestone likes him much either . . . not after this morning.'

Dan had an unnerving glimpse into a muddled grown-up world where magistrates and policemen could make the most ghastly mistakes.

'Well, if they charge him,' he said at last. 'I'll tell my grandfather all about Kevin Britton. My grandfather wouldn't allow anyone to be unjustly punished. I know he wouldn't. . . .'

Then, longing for Henry's approval, he added:

'. . . Will that do?'

Henry gave him a slow smile.

'It's better than nothing,' he said.

As they passed the old brickworks on their way back to the Danestone road, Dan got off his bicycle.

'What are you stopping for?'

'Getting rid of this,' he replied, screwing the copy of the 'East Anglian Sunday News' into a tight ball and shoving it far down a rabbit hole.

It was good to think of all evidence of the horrible boy lying buried three feet under the earth.

5
Monday

Next morning Dan awoke to a summer haze. The tennis lawn and the rockery and his grandmother's border looked as though shrouded in dust sheets, awaiting a spring-clean. He gazed up at the muffled sky and knew what it meant: yet another scorching day. By ten or eleven o'clock there would not be a cloud to be seen and this cloaking mist would have dwindled and changed into the shimmering heat-devils dancing a foot above the tarmac roads. He lay back in the camp-bed smiling with contentment. It was going to be perfect Suffolk weather – and he had three whole days of Henry entirely to himself. His cousins, poor idiots, would be sailing up and down the Waveney with their father all today and Tuesday and Wednesday in the races at Rushby Regatta. He and Henry were free to do anything they liked. Even the memory of Kevin Britton could not dim his pleasure for he – Dan – had confessed himself to Henry. He felt curiously absolved and no longer responsible for what he had done. Besides, Kevin Britton had taken himself off. The whole matter was finished, stuffed out of sight down that rabbit-hole, at Wainstead brickworks. It could stay there for ever and ever – or until a mother rabbit started chewing it up to make a nest with.

In this last he was soon to be disappointed.

Coming in to breakfast half an hour later, he glanced over his grandfather's shoulder as he passed behind his chair and saw Kevin Britton scowling up at him from the front page of 'The Times'.

'Dan, I'm so sorry,' his grandmother was saying. 'I'm getting so forgetful. First it's the milk and now it's the cornflakes. I was so sure I'd bought another packet. But I must have left it in the shop.'

'It doesn't matter a bit,' he heard himself murmur, thinking with half his mind: 'She's getting very old'; and with the other half wondering anxiously how long it would take his grandfather to reach the Borstal boy.

'Boil him an extra egg,' the old man said without taking his eyes off the paper.

'How long is it going to be?' Dan asked himself as he sat down at the table and began squinting nervously at the list of births, marriages, and deaths on the back page.

Then he noted the direction of his grandfather's eyes. They were now levelled straight at the boy's photograph. Now he was reading the story that went below.

'Well, Madge,' he suddenly burst out. 'Here's devil's work! *That* you can't deny. Look at this miserable piece of humanity.'

Dan's grandmother came over and stood behind him, the egg for boiling balanced inexpertly in a spoon in her hand.

'He looks very young, dear,' she said.

'The young scoundrel's not yet seventeen.'

'And he looks very intelligent. What's he done?'

'Exploded a gun straight into a policeman's face.'

Dan let out a gasp of horror. The 'East Anglian Sunday News' had not put it as starkly as that.

'Has he blown off his head?' he asked in a voice near to panic.

His grandfather picked up the paper and scanned the story again, a look of perplexity creasing his brows, while Dan, his heart thumping with terror, wondered whether he had given his grandmother's chicken stew to a murderer. But the boy *couldn't* have killed a policeman. The 'East Anglian Sunday News' would have said so. The newspaper placard outside Ma Mavers' shop would have blared out 'Hunt for a Killer'.

'The young constable's injured and off duty,' his grandfather said, looking up from the paper. 'But he can't be dangerously hurt. He's not even been admitted to hospital.'

'That's very odd, isn't it?' said his grandmother, doing her egg and spoon race back to the stove and the saucepan of boiling water. 'You'd have thought that he'd at least have shot off an ear.'

'You're being very casual, Madge,' exclaimed his grandfather angrily. 'This brutal young thug's been letting off firearms in the face of the law.'

'No dear. No dear, I'm not,' she replied in some distress. 'It's dreadful what he's done. It's . . . it's just that I'm trying to see how it was.'

'Why on earth did he shoot in the first place?'

'Perhaps he was frightened,' Dan blurted out.

'*Frightened?*' his grandfather exploded. 'And don't you think that poor young constable was frightened, too?'

Dan looked up startled. He had never thought of policemen being frightened. They looked so safe and buttoned-up and protected with their helmets and their truncheons and the whole weight of society behind them.

'You young people don't understand,' the old man thundered. 'Law and order are sacred. *Sacred*. Without law and order we'd be back behaving like the cavemen. We'd go beating our neighbours over their heads for their last chunk of raw meat. And if law and order are sacred, why then, so are policemen. They protect us from chaos.'

Dan forgave him his wrath. He realised gropingly that it was not so much himself that his grandfather was castigating; it was Nick. In the heat of the moment he must have forgotten that Nick was dead.

'Where did all this happen?' asked his grandmother from the stove.

'Near where your Aunt Lily used to live. At Higham Ferrers.'

'Aunt Lily? Good gracious. Well that's miles and miles away.'

'Yes, but they think he's heading this way.'

'What, towards us here at Danestone?'

'No. No. No. Not towards Danestone especially. They think he's somewhere in East Anglia.'

'And he's a thief? Escaped from Borstal?'

'Yes.'

'Then I think I'll just give Philippa a ring to tell George to lock up all that silver.'

Though breakfast was darkened by the long shadow of Kevin Britton and his crimes, the rest of that August Monday was pure joy. It was a jewel of a day, for late in the morning an event occurred in Danestone so astonishing and so beautiful that all thoughts of the world's wickedness were swallowed up in its glory. Quite simply, it was the day that the road between Danestone and Thursby caught fire.

Dan and Henry and Jim were far down on the marsh fishing in the quiet and shady reach just above the lock. It was so hot that nothing in nature moved save the maggots wriggling about in Jim's rusty tin. Not a breath of wind stirred the trees or the reeds, and the glassy water of the river reflected the sky as unblinkingly as a mirror. A fisherman's silence had caught the three of them,

a silence so compelling that Henry, who knew nothing about fishing and who was longing to know what they were supposed to be at, felt awed into holding his tongue. Obediently, he held Nick's rod straight out in front of him and watched the stupid float sticking up doing nothing at all and wondered what pleasure anyone could find in such a tedious sport. He glanced sideways at the others. They looked as though a wizard had muttered an incantation and frozen up their blood.

At last, a little wind whispering down the river ruffled up the water, sent the three floats bobbing, and broke the spell.

Jim reeled in his line with a clatter and then cast again.

'We'll get a bite in a minute, yew'll see,' he said encouragingly.

'But I don't see the point of catching the fish,' burst out Henry. 'Not if they're so muddy-tasting that they're not worth eating.'

'It's just for the fun of it,' said Dan.

'Gar'n,' jeered Jim. 'It's to get bait.'

'Bait? Bait for what?'

'The ole pike up in t'pool,' and he jerked his head upstream.

Pike were worth a mint of money, he explained, if one took the trouble to bicycle them the ten miles up the valley to the restaurant at Brockdish. The cook there turned them into something French and posh people drove for miles to eat the stuff.

'Got a whole quid for the last pike I caught,' he

said with a grin. 'And it's quite legal, too, now I've got meself a licence.'

Silence descended upon them all again as the ruffling breeze blew away downstream and the river resumed its bland calm. But the spell was broken. Henry sighed with relief. He felt free to take his eyes off his float and gaze about him. River. Reeds. Sky. Underwater green depths. And rat-holes in the bank. It was pleasant really, in a queer mud-smelling sort of way. It might be pleasanter, he thought, catching pike for pocket-money here in this emptiness than trudging the streets of Ealing on a paper round as he had done all last winter holidays. A boy could be on his own down on this marsh. Be his own master. All the same, he grumbled to himself as the silence lengthened and the floats continued to remain motionless in the slack of the tide, one had to wait an awful long time in these parts for anything to happen.

Then he turned his head and gazed behind him back across the green marshes they had traversed to the low line of Danestone village, its pantile roofs strung out along the horizon, the odd, round tower of its flint church sticking up on its slight hill at the far end. Something in the sky over the village caught his attention and he stared on, watching a faint grey haze beneath the August blue darken and then turn on its underside to a tawny brown.

'I think that's a fire!' he exclaimed excitedly, pointing towards Danestone.

Dan looked round.

'Yes. It is,' he said.

Jim, his attention called away from a nibble on his line, glanced round quickly and then returned to business.

'They're burning the stubble. Thet's all.'

'Why?' asked Henry, not taking his eyes off the changing smudge in the sky. 'Why do they burn the stubble?'

'It's to kill the bugs, I think,' Dan volunteered. 'Or else to clear the fields. The combine harvesters can't cut very close, you know. They do it every year.'

And he returned, like Jim, to his fishing. For the two of them it was the end of the affair.

But not for Henry. Henry continued to stand with his back to the river, Nick's rod dangling idly in his hand, gazing enraptured at the pall of smoke hanging in the sky beyond the village. Anything alight had always entranced him, anything from a guttering candle to a bonfire and from a bonfire to a blazing house. The flames seemed to light him up and make him feel like a king. They set something free inside him that felt wild and brave and wonderful. As he watched, a light wind began shaking the willow leaves over his head and a stronger wind on the far side of Danestone sent the smoke from the stubble fire spiralling high into the zenith. He looked back at his two companions crouched on the bank still intent on their fishing and longed to be off across the marsh. Mere stubble-burning or no, he longed to be as close as he possibly could to the fire that was causing all that smoke. When he turned back to gaze through the willow trunks once more, he saw flames leaping high into the pall.

'Look!' he shouted. 'That can't just be stubble.'

The others turned, stood up, and stared with him.

'Crikey!' gasped Dan.

'Thet's a right ole fire and no mistake,' Jim admitted with a generous grin.

At that moment, in the stillness, came the hurried clanging of a bell, faint at first and then disappearing and then growing louder.

'It's a *real* fire!' Dan shouted, jumping up and down. 'That's the Rushby fire-engine.'

'Come on,' cried Jim, reeling up his shrieking line. 'Come on.'

And he plunged off through the trees and out across the marsh, holding his rod out in front of him like a charging pikeman. Earlier that morning the three of them had walked, like all other sensible fishermen, along the lane which led from the village to Barlingham Lock, but this lane – in true Suffolk fashion – skirted three sides round a grazing to avoid the winter quagmires. Jim, as excited now as Henry, had no time for such slowness. Dan and Henry followed in his wake, jumping from tussock to tussock and stumbling over the deeply pocked turf where, in wetter weather, the cows had churned up the clay.

'It's very difficult,' panted Dan, having fallen flat on his face, and now picking himself up quickly.

'Look where yew're goin',' Jim shouted back over his shoulder.

'I can't,' Dan muttered.

At the best of times, the ground at his feet was in a haze; and now he had dust and grass-seed all over his glasses.

'Give me your hand,' Henry said, grasping him firmly. 'I'll swing you over this dike. It looks flatter on the other side.'

They ran on blindly, drawn by the fire as frantically as a herd of wild animals aware of a salt-lick. They were drawing near the village now; they could see the runner beans growing up their pole wigwams in the back-gardens and the Mobbs family underwear hanging out to dry. Better still, the smell of the fire was now pricking the back of their noses.

They came to a halt at last at Mr Fenton's six-bar gate and caught their breath.

'Listen!' said Henry, straining his ears over the bumping going on in his chest. 'Can you hear it?'

The three of them stood as quietly as they could, and over the cackling of the hens and a man shouting in the village street and the growing clamour of the fire-engine came the distant but unmistakable roar of the flames.

'Goodness!' exclaimed Dan, filled with a pleasurable awe.

'It's good, all right!' grinned Jim. 'The fire's up on the Thursby road. It might burn down the p'liceman's house.'

Then, scrambling over the gate, they ran along Fenton's Lane and out into the village street.

Danestone was deserted. It was the middle of the summer holidays yet there was not a child to be seen. Even The Jolly Boatman's black labrador, always asleep in the dust outside the public bar, had woken up and trotted off elsewhere.

'Where's everyone gone?' shouted Dan as he galloped up the street.

'To t'fire,' called out Mrs Mobbs, who had suddenly appeared, standing in her shop door. 'Yew're late.'

It sounded like a taunt. The three passed her; but then Dan stopped and ran back.

'Will you take care of our fishing-rods, Mrs Mobbs?' he panted.

'Put 'em among t'brooms,' she said with a nod.

He and Henry parked them outside the shop among the household gear, and Jim, glancing over his shoulder, stopped, ran back, and did the same.

'Come on,' he cried impatiently to the others as he hurtled on up the street.

'Jim, bor, don't yew run them two into no trouble,' Mrs Mobbs shouted after him.

''Corse not,' he yelled back.

'There's no 'corse, at all – not with yew, Jim Foulger,' she bawled up the silent street.

The insult fell on deaf ears, for the fire had the three of them in thrall. As Henry saw that the smoke was now darkening half the sky, he grinned all over his face. It was a huger and more wonderful fire than he had ever dreamed possible. They were late, late, late, thought Dan, gasping along in the rear. They were sure to be missing the best of it. 'Burn, burn, burn,' prayed Jim with the savagery of an Old Testament prophet. 'Burn everything down.' It was the just reward for a village which had brought him to disgrace. They could not yet see the flames for the field ablaze must lie on the far side of the upper road, hidden from Danestone Street by the slight hill on which stood the church, the vicarage, and the policeman's house. But the roar of the fire now sounded wild, dangerous, and quite close, and the air was growing warm about their faces. Dan looked up for a second at the smoke swirling up over the lip of the low hill and felt something soft and light brushing against his cheek; and then again and again until something grey and fragile landed on his glasses.

'It's ash!' he shouted to Henry. 'It's like feathers. It's coming down all round us.'

'Up Church Lane,' Jim yelled back at them, as he wheeled left and disappeared behind the tall hedgerow.

In Church Lane everything was pandemonium. The Rushby fire-engine had come to a halt wedged between the Danestone–Rushby bus and the steep bank of the lane. The firemen and the bus-driver were shouting abuse at each other.

'The bus's broken down,' Jim explained as the other two caught up with him. 'They can't get it started.'

Henry's grin grew even wider. With no hose pipes, the fire could have its day. Besides, through the tangle of bus and fire-engine he had caught his first sight of the blazing hedge at the far end of the lane.

'Come on,' he shouted. 'If we climb up the

bank and push through the hedge, perhaps we can get along by a field or something.'

'The churchyard,' said Dan.

''Corse,' said Jim, putting action to words.

Among the tombs, Dan met his Aunt Philippa with a bucket in her hand.

'The church thatch,' she moaned. 'The church thatch. We've got to save the thatch.'

She was running towards the tap where the mourners filled their vases for the graves.

Dan cursed his ill-luck. Here was a duty running slap up against his pleasure. But then he caught sight of the vicar in gum-boots hurrying up with his wife's fish kettle and, behind him, the grave-digger trundling a wheelbarrow containing two huge watering-cans.

'I've got through to them, Mrs Heseltine,' the Vicar shouted to Aunt Philippa. 'Told them about the bus. They're sending more fire-engines to us along the upper road. From Rushby. From Bungay. From Loddon. They've even alerted Lowestoft.'

Dan sighed with relief. There was no need for him to stop. There were adults and help enough. He could slip by quickly and join the others. Henry, at the far end of the churchyard, also heard the Vicar's shout and exulted in his heart. Three fire-engines – and perhaps more! Something quite stupendous must lie just ahead. Then he was scrambling up the high brick wall beyond the farthest hummocks of the most ancient graves with Jim at his side, just as a tremendous shout went up from the boys and girls of Danestone crowding up on top of Mr Fenton's muck heap on the opposite side of Church Lane.

'Et's caught!' cried a boy.

'Et's ablaze,' cried another.

'Et'll set alight to all the rest,' screeched a girl.

Henry and Jim, now astride the wall, gazed below them with astonished joy. The whole of Mr Fenton's forty-acre field lay striped and blackened from end to end, smouldering with little ribs of fire still running along the lines of stubble. It was a huge devastation. But what lay closer at hand was better still. A hundred yards of the hedge along the far side of the Thursby road was sputtering and crackling in a wall of flame, while to the right of them some sixty feet away the gaunt skeleton of a dead elm tree was flaring like a mighty torch.

'She's right,' Henry shouted, though Jim was only a foot away. 'When the flames reach the end of the branches they'll leap to the elm next door.'

'And wi' a bit o' wind,' Jim shouted back, 'they'll leap t'road and set 'em alight down this side, too.'

The thought of the Thursby road running a gauntlet of fire filled them with awe. Just a little wind – just a very little wind – would do the trick. Henry gazed across the blackened field and gave a startled gasp, for under the far hedge the lines of charred stubble were glowing brightly and now bursting into little creeping fires. The little wind was on its way. Sitting there on top of the wall watching the embers stir to life and the smoke flatten and drift towards them, he felt suddenly uncomfortably out of sorts. It was unnerving to know that by wishing something one could make it happen.

'Where's Dan?' he asked, by way of distraction.

They looked back over their shoulders across the long churchyard at a knot of people gathered round a ladder propped against the wall of the church and Mrs Heseltine, weighed down by her bucket, returning from the tap.

'Dunno,' said Jim, turning back to the blazing elm tree. 'He always were some 'un to get left behind.'

Poor Dan had not been able to make the escape that he had prayed for. The Vicar, fish-kettle and all, had borne down on him with an immediate plea for help.

'Dan, you're the very person I've been looking for.'

'Me?' Dan could hardly believe this. And he didn't *want* to believe it, either. He wanted to be off after Henry.

'You can climb a ladder? You can scramble about on that roof?'

And Mr Micklethwaite pointed to the thatch over the nave.

'Yes . . . yes . . . I think I can.'

He looked at the thatch and at the air above it thick with the flying motes of ash from the fire. At any other time he would have been overjoyed to have been asked to fool about on top of the church.

'Well, I want you up there quick with my rose syringe.'

Dan looked at him utterly bewildered.

'Your rose syringe?'

'It's the best thing I can think of. We'll bring you the water . . . and all you've got to do is to scramble about squirting it wherever you see a spark alight. It's . . . it's only until the fire-engines arrive.'

Dan looked longingly past the Vicar at his two friends sitting on the wall with the sky beyond them shot with lurid, flaring light. . . . But he was caught. Hopelessly caught. There was nothing he could do.

He was hurried to the foot of the ladder and handed the syringe. Filling it at Aunt Philippa's bucket, he tried it out and squirted her straight in the bosom by mistake. Then, having got the hang of the thing, he refilled it and mounted up on high.

It was much better fun on top of the thatch than he had thought it would be, for he could look far down the Thursby road and see the full extent of the fire. He saw the vast, smouldering field and the elm tree blazing away like a huge candelabra not far from Henry and Jim, but he could also see round the corner of the road where three elm trees together were roaring to heaven in a perfect inferno. There was little time, however, for fire-gazing. The flakes of ash were now falling about him in a grey snowstorm and some of them fell hot on his face and hands. He squirted the water hurriedly about him and then scrambled down to the eaves to fill up.

'Is anything smouldering?' shouted the Vicar.

'Not so as I can see,' he panted. 'But the ash's hot.'

More grown-ups had turned up in the churchyard: Mr Mobbs, Mr Fenton, Mrs Micklethwaite, the Heseltine's gardener. And then, as he scrambled higher, he caught sight of his grandparents – returned from Norwich – coming through the lych-gate. He was glad they'd come back. It felt better with them there. Back on the roof ridge, he looked down below his right foot and saw that the thatch was beginning to smoulder. He squirted the water and then began to panic, for the reeds were still smoking. The rose syringe was no good. He wanted a whole bucket. Lots of buckets.

'It's smoking, Mr Micklethwaite, round here on the other side,' he bawled down. 'I want much more water.'

Henry, meantime, worried about Dan and, in truth, finding sitting on the wall far too hot for comfort, had slithered back into the churchyard and was running towards the church. And Jim, intrigued by what was going on among the grown-ups, was following close on his heels. Both arrived at the foot of the ladder just as Dan gave his cry for help.

'Let me go up to him, sir,' said Henry, turning to the Vicar. 'I'm good at heights.'

And without waiting for an answer, he seized a watering-can out of the grave-digger's hands and raced up the ladder.

'Me, too,' growled Jim.

'Of course. Of course,' murmured Mr Micklethwaite in the fluster of the moment. Then, recognising that it was his blasphemous ex-choirboy who was so manfully shouldering his fish-kettle up on to the roof, he gave a wry smile. The Almighty certainly had strange ways of bringing a sinner to redemption.

'Here. Here,' shouted Dan, pointing to the smouldering patch of reed.

'That's not smoke, you ass,' Henry panted. 'It's . . . it's steam.'

But he tipped the whole watering-can over it all the same. Then they looked hurriedly about them for trouble elsewhere.

'Gi' me a hand wi' this bloody thing,' yelled Jim from the top of the ladder. The fish-kettle was all the wrong shape for carrying and roof-climbing at the same time.

Dan slithered down to help him.

'Over there. Near the tower,' shouted Henry, spread-eagled for the moment as he hurried sideways to beat out a fresh spark.

Down in the churchyard, the adult parishioners of St Felix, Danestone, had formed themselves into a human chain. Dan's Aunt Philippa filled the buckets and cans at the tap and passed them to Colonel Henchman and he to the gravedigger and the gravedigger to Mr Fenton and so on right down the line to the Vicar, now half-way up the ladder. Only Dan's grandmother stood idle. She looked up at her grandson hopping and slithering about on the roof under the pall of ash and mentally wrung her hands. She could not bear it. She had lost one grandson already.

'It's not safe for the boy,' she whispered to her husband. 'It's not safe.'

Colonel Henchman looked up startled, then took time off for a moment to watch the three boys jumping about and laughing as they sloshed the water over the reed thatch of his parish church.

'Nonsense, Madge. They're having the time of their lives.' Then, since she still looked in anguish, he added: 'Come now, if it *does* get too hot for them up there, all they've got to do is to slide down. Not one of them'll get anything worse than a bump on the bottom.'

Deeply anxious though he was to save his church, the danger to the boys had penetrated Mr Micklethwaite's mind as well.

'You must come down if you think it's not safe,' he told Henry, as he handed him up his wife's coal scuttle filled with blackened water.

'It's all right, sir. Anyhow for the moment. We're getting it properly soaked.'

But he spoke too soon.

'Quick. Quick,' bellowed Jim, hurling down an empty bucket and scrambling towards the join between the thatch over the nave and the red pantiles which roofed the chancel. 'It's alight over our screen.'

St Felix's painted rood screen was the pride of the parish. It was mentioned in Pevsner.

Ripping off the first thing that he came to, he tried to smother the flames with his old fishing jacket. Then Henry and Dan came up with the coal scuttle.

'God, I hope that does it,' Jim groaned as the steam hissed up fiercely all about them.

'I'm moving the ladder,' shouted the Vicar.

'Moving it closer to the three of you.'

At this moment everything happened at once. Mrs Micklethwaite, who had run into the church belatedly remembering that there were two Tudor leather fire buckets hanging up in the vestry, ran out again, shouting:

'Jasper, Jasper, the plaster's sagging. Water's dripping through into the pulpit.'

'Water?' barked the Vicar. 'There's worse things than water.'

Water was their salvation . . . if there was to *be* a salvation.

And here it came at last – with the clanging of the fire-engines approaching from Bungay along the upper road and from the shouts of the Rushby crew who had finally disentangled themselves from the broken-down bus. The firemen had opened a hydrant at the top of Church Lane and were now running their hoses between the tombs.

Last, but not least, Dan, standing on the church roof watching entranced as the hoses began to thicken with water – and heedless to the shouts to come down, felt himself to his consternation slowly disappearing downwards. He gave a startled yell and clutched at the charred reeds; but it was too late. Feet foremost, he fell through the thatch and the sagging ceiling and landed in a smother of plaster inside the pulpit.

'Dan, Dan,' cried his grandmother, running into the church and down the nave. 'Dan, darling, are you all right?'

Dan was not quite sure how he was. He felt

jarred and angry, thinking – as well he might – that roofs shouldn't behave in such an unpredictable way. But where he was or what he was doing he could not imagine. He could see nothing at all; his glasses were coated with wet plaster. He groped about him with scratched hands and found he was standing upright in a very large, tall box.

'Where am I?' he croaked, his throat dry from the charred reed dust and the flying plaster.

'It's all right, darling. You're in the pulpit. I'm coming up.'

And in a moment, he smelt her lavender smell, and she was taking off his fogged glasses and making little noises like a mother hen.

Dan, deciding that there was nothing much the matter with him, squinted about him, first at his grandmother cleaning his glasses on her handkerchief, then at the terrible mess all about them, and finally up above his head.

'Oh goodness!' he gasped in horror, for through the great hole in the ceiling he could see the sky. 'Look what I've done! They'll be terribly angry.'

'I don't think they will, dear,' replied his grandmother. 'You did your best.'

They got themselves out of the pulpit just in time for as Dan was walking somewhat shakily down the nave at his grandmother's side, a shoot of water from the Rushby hoses fell like a cloudburst through the hole in the roof and drenched where they had stood.

'Dan, are you all right?' shouted Henry running into the church. Then, seeing that his friend was at least walking, he added: 'Come quickly. The Bungay firemen are wearing masks. And something extraordinary's happened. *The road's on fire!*'

Dan, his glasses back on his nose, stumbled hurriedly off after Henry, his grandmother, the smouldering thatch, and the hole in the roof all forgotten in favour of this eighth wonder of the world.

'Is the boy all right?' he heard his grandfather shout across the churchyard.

Yet so ravishing were the elm trees blazing away beyond the brick wall and the thought of the tarmac on fire that he wondered hazily to whom his grandfather was referring.

'Where's Jim?' he gasped.

'Up on the wall,' replied Henry. 'Can't you see him?'

And there, sure enough, was a familiar pair of shoulders, hunched and dark against the backcloth of the flames.

Once up on the wall himself, Dan found the heat intolerable. It came at him like a breath from his namesake's fiery furnace. But he saw the masked firemen running up with their hoses, eerie and faceless like the T.V. spacemen; he saw the tarmac cracking and bubbling and licked with bluish flames; he heard the frantic bells of the fire-engines coming in from Loddon and Rushby. And then, happy but defeated, he slipped off the wall back into the churchyard and was violently sick.

'Are you all right?' asked Henry, looking back over his shoulder.

'Yes. Yes. Quite all right,' he smiled whitely. 'It's just the heat.'

It wasn't as bad as it might have been, he thought with relief. His long-ago breakfast had hidden itself discreetly in a bed of nettles.

'It's too hot for me,' Henry admitted.

'We'll get over into Mr Fenton's cabbages,' said Jim, jerking his head up the Thursby road. 'We can watch it all from farther away.'

So the three of them got through the wire fence which separated the churchyard from the great field of blue cabbages and stood and watched the battle afar off. They saw the jets of water playing over the flaring elms and reducing them to blackened gallows; they saw the magical road turned to sodden cinders. They watched beauty sputter and steam and stink and die away.

'Et's not touched the p'liceman's house,' growled Jim as they began trailing home.

'Nor the Vicarage,' said Dan.

'And the church roof looks as though it's now safe,' remarked Henry.

The crew of the first Rushby fire-engine had come down from the thatch and was now coiling up the hoses.

Dan sighed. He felt sated with pleasure.

'It was good fun,' he smiled.

'Won't Peter and Nigel be mad to have missed it!' grinned Henry.

'Sick as mud,' agreed Dan happily.

On their way down Danestone Street to pick up their fishing-rods, they were overtaken by two police cars slowly patrolling the village.

'They've come a bit late in the day,' said Henry scornfully.

'Why?' asked Dan. 'Policemen don't put out fires.'

'They go and poke their noses into who's started 'em,' said Jim sourly.

'But nobody started *this* fire, surely?' exclaimed Henry. 'It just happened.'

'Me Uncle Ed . . . he's Mr Fenton's field hand. Et's he that'll 've fired the stubble.'

'And he'll get into trouble?'

''Corse he will,' replied Jim grimly. 'Get the sack very like.'

Later, the two friends watched him, rod in hand, clump down the lane towards his mother's cottage, surly and defiant once more. They saw that for him, at least, the glory of the day had departed.

But as they got back to The Old House, they soon found that it had certainly not departed for themselves.

'Well done,' Dan's grandfather greeted them. 'You've saved the church roof.'

'We're all very proud of you,' said his grandmother, and then added, laughing: 'But goodness, you look like chimney sweeps . . . and darlings, you smell like them, too. Go and have a bath.'

Dan glanced at Henry in embarrassment. His grandmother had an absolute passion for baths. He hoped that Henry did not think she was too odd.

'Was the Vicar very cross about that hole?' he called back at her as he trailed up the stairs.

'Of course not,' she shouted up from the kitchen. 'They're getting a tarpaulin up over it this afternoon.'

So far from being cross was the Vicar that he rang up at tea-time and asked if Dan and Henry would accompany them to the Rushby fair on Tuesday night. It was the annual choirboys' outing.

'Is Jim going too?' Dan asked.

'Dan asks if you're taking Jim Foulger, too,' said his grandmother into the telephone. 'You are? Good. Well, I know they'd love to go. Thank you, Jasper. At the Vicarage at eight? They'll be there.'

'*Two* visits to the fair!' exclaimed Dan, overwhelmed at the sudden extravagance of grown-ups.

'Of course,' said his grandfather, smiling his crooked smile. 'We'll go on Wednesday as well. We can't miss the fireworks.'

6
Tuesday

THE great stubble fire was an event so huge and magnificent that it blocked out the past and set a new complexion on the future. It was like the Battle of Hastings in 1066. The people who had been important only the day before yesterday were cast into oblivion. Kevin Britton was utterly forgotten. History had swallowed him up. Even Simon and Nigel had dwindled to mere Saxons. These two – poor idiots – had watched the fire from three miles away, captive spectators caught in the doldrums in a race in the middle of the Waveney. They had cursed their luck bitterly. Without a breath of wind in their sails, they could neither leave the race and sail up the river nor yet get to the bank and scramble ashore. Once home, and hearing of Dan and Henry's feat and the Vicar's kindly reward, they had burst out in fury.

'It's not fair!' Nigel had railed. 'If we'd been here we could've done just as well.'

'He's right,' Simon had backed him up. 'There's nothing much to scrambling about on the church roof. Any fool could've done it if he'd only been there.'

Their father had tried to calm them. He'd take them, he said, on their own to the fair on Tuesday night. They didn't really want to be cumbered with the Danestone choirboys, did they? They'd have much better fun on their own.

But it wasn't the same – and they both knew it. That little twirp Dan had stolen a march on them – and dragged their friend Henry along with him.

The stubble fire, however, not only blotted out the past, it also hurried on the future. Any great event draws those who take part in it close together; and the fewer of them that there are the closer are the bonds. Dan, who might have taken a month to feel completely safe with Henry, greeted him next morning as the friend of a life-time. He was his boon companion; his other self. He felt sure that it was even safe enough to take Henry up to the attic.

So, though the sun was still pouring down outside, the two of them spent the first hour of that Tuesday morning close up under the roof-tiles in the agreeable, shut-up fug of his grandparents' lumber-room, poking about in the drawers of birds' eggs, riffling through the hundreds of foreign stamps, and finally running down to the kitchen and up again with a box of matches to light one of the little cones of incense which Great-Uncle Bob had brought back with him from India. Dan was immensely proud of his forbears and the strange junk they had left behind; but both made him also feel oddly protective. He could not bear that anyone should laugh at them.

He soon saw that he need have no fear with Henry. Henry confessed that he knew almost nothing about his own family: that his parents, for all he had been told, had arrived on this planet without either fathers or mothers or even brothers and sisters. They had always appeared to him utterly rootless and without a past. Therefore, Dan's Great-Uncle Timothy's boomerang brought back from Queensland and Dan's Great-Grandfather's bayonet left over from the First World War were not only a delight in themselves but also added greatly to his new friend's stature. They made Dan belong somewhere, made this family who were being so kind to him, feel a part of history. And Henry was clever enough to be impressed.

'How wonderful to have ancestors who've been to places and done things,' he sighed. 'I wish I had.'

Dan was pleased. 'Ancestors' seemed a very grand word for his grandfather's forbears. But he was also a little perplexed for, though there in the attic lay all the odd things that they had gathered from the ends of the world and had so thoughtfully left behind, he was not quite sure what any of these worthies had actually *done*. Had they been missionaries or merchants or soldiers or gold-diggers – or what? There was only one of his forbears that he knew anything exciting about and that was his grandfather's great-great grandfather, who had fought at Trafalgar. He glanced at Henry. Should he tell him about his family's great hero? He decided not. It was too huge a boast. He'd be as bad as his cousins bragging about their wealth.

'Take the censer,' he said instead, handing

Henry the silver casket puffing with incense. 'Swing it about and pretend you're a Buddhist priest.'

So Henry grasped the silver chains and went round the long attic, swinging the censer solemnly at the case of Jamaican butterflies, at the trunks of ancient clothes, at the stamps and the bayonet and the boomerang, and at a dusty topee hanging on a peg, muttering unintelligible blessings in what he hoped was Siamese, and came finally to a halt beside his friend.

'Now it's your turn,' he said with a grin. 'And mind you give your blessing in that Chinese you learn at school.'

It was a strange interlude in those extraordinary five days.

By mid-morning they had grown tired of the attic. The place stank of incense, dust, and dead flies. Besides, it had grown far too hot. So, stubbing out the smouldering cone and throwing it into the cold-water tank, they clattered down the back stairs and out into the kitchen garden in search of the last raspberries.

'I liked that,' said Henry, as they stooped down between the towering rows of canes.

'Liked what?'

'Seeing all those things up there. . . .'

Dan put a handful of raspberries into his mouth and, crushing them against his palate, felt that life was good.

'And now,' continued Henry quietly. 'I'd like to see inside those maltings.'

'Inside the maltings?' Dan exclaimed in alarm. 'But . . . they're out of bounds. I . . . I told you so.'

Not only were they out of bounds but he also now hated them. His last visit there, when the fierce boy had jumped out and grabbed him, had given him a terrible fright.

'Out of bounds because they're dangerous,' Henry argued. 'But you went into them . . . and they didn't fall down. . . .'

Dan rather wished that they had. The maltings had lost all their magic. They were defiled, somehow. And shaming. They were now only a place where he had been horribly afraid. He didn't *want* to go back to them. Besides, he didn't want to anger his grandfather. Why should he? The old man had been so proud of them after the fire. Why go and spoil it?

'. . . I don't see how it can really do any harm,' continued Henry in his sensible way. 'We won't fool about. . . . .'

He'd just like to see where he and Nick used to play, he explained. And where Dan had come upon the Borstal boy.

'. . . Of course, if you're afraid . . . or don't want to go . . . or something . . . I could always go on my own.'

Dan glanced at his companion's pleasant, ugly face with the raspberry stains round its mouth and thought in perplexity that, for one's very best friend, Henry could make one feel very uncomfortable at times. Down on Wainstead Staithe on Sunday afternoon, he had made him feel ashamed for not having done the right thing; and now here, in the raspberries, he was suggesting that he was a coward for not doing something wrong. He stood up and gazed through the straggly tops of the canes in order to sort things out, and saw the warm brick walls of his grandparents' house glowing in the August sunlight. The house meant peace to him – and affection. But his eyes travelled on up to the cobwebby window of the attic where they had just been. What would his ancestors think of him, he wondered, if they could look down at him in his dilemma. Would the owners of the topee and the bayonet and the boomerang dismiss him as a coward? Would the boy who was his hero – the powder-monkey at Trafalgar – jeer at him as a frightened child? The answer made up his mind,

'All right,' he muttered reluctantly. 'We'll go this afternoon.'

His grandparents were driving over to Loddon garden-centre soon after two. They had told him at breakfast.

After all, he thought, as he stooped to pick more raspberries, perhaps it was better to lay a ghost and push Kevin Britton out of his life once for all.

To get through the time till lunch, they wandered up the village street to Mrs Mobbs to buy chewing-gum; gum-chewing, they had discovered, being something much frowned upon both by Henry's mother and Dan's parents. Neither liked the stuff very much, but slurping it about inside their mouths made a sort of peace-pact. It made up in some strange ways for the visit to the maltings.

On the way back they were passed by yet another police car.

'I wonder what's happened to Jim's Uncle Ed,' said Dan between chews. 'You couldn't go to prison for a thing like that, could you?'

'Not if it was an accident,' replied the all-knowing Henry. 'Besides, it wasn't as though anyone was killed.'

No. No one had been killed, thought Dan. But the whole village still stank of the fire. The raw, sharp smell of the burnt trees and the soaked tarmac hung heavy in the air, and up on the hill stood the church with a great hole in its poor, sodden roof. If a boy for a prank had done so much damage, he'd be in terrible trouble with the police.

'Hi, yew. . . .' came a shout from Jim's lane.

And they turned and saw Jim running up towards them.

'. . . Yew goin' to t'fair tonight?'

They nodded and grinned. Dan saw that Jim was surprisingly himself again: the Jim of last summer; the Jim they had both met at the setting up of the fair.

'We're all meeting at the Vicarage at eight,' said Henry.

'Bit of all right,' remarked their friend with his slow Suffolk smile. 'And that fire were a bit of all right, too.'

How were things with his uncle, they both asked.

Even he was all right, he replied. He'd had a rocket from Mr Fenton and a proper dressing-down from the fire-brigade. But the police hadn't been near him. And he still had his job.

'He didn't look for such luck,' Jim admitted. 'We're not a lucky fam'ly, we aren't.'

A second police car passed them.

'Well, if it's all right,' asked Henry with a puzzled air, 'why are all these fuzzes buzzing about?'

Jim shrugged his shoulders. Perhaps they had found the thief who had broken into Ma Mavers', he suggested. He showed no glimmer of interest. In his happy mood, other people's crimes didn't bother him much. But, looking at his two friends working away with their jaws, he wouldn't have minded a chew.

'Gi' me a bit,' he said.

'Sorry,' exclaimed Dan, surprised by his own bad manners.

And he hastily pulled out a long ribbon of wet gum.

'Here you are,' he said, breaking off a gob.

And the three of them dawdled on down the street in the hot sunshine, ruminating in silence – and marvellously at peace with the world.

Three hours later, Henry and Dan waved the old people good-bye as they drove off to Loddon, and then, looking nervously about them, feeling that the empty old house and the cedar tree and the tennis lawn were disapproving witnesses of their misdoing, they slipped through the gate in the wall and out into Fenton's Lane and made towards the weed-mantled head of the Danestone dike. Ahead of them basked the maltings.

Once out of the glare of the day and into the cool shadows of the maltster's den, Henry exclaimed at the smell.

'Goodness!' he said loudly. 'What a very odd stink.'

Dan was appalled. It was like shouting aloud in church. No. It was worse than that. Far worse. Remembering his last visit, the maltings seemed to him full of menace. Some unknown terror was waiting to pounce out on them and catch them up and strangle them with crooked fingers of steel. Looking about him in this darkened lower floor and listening to the emptiness in the floor above, he wanted to hide himself in silence – as he hid himself in bed from the terror that stalked by night. 'Don't move. Don't breathe,' he'd told himself time and time again. 'The horror'll pass you by. It won't know where you are.'

'. . . What ever is it?' Henry pursued. 'It smells like an old railway-station on a wet day.'

'Shut up,' whispered Dan urgently. 'You don't want everyone to hear we're here.'

'But there's no one about,' Henry replied in a hoarse mutter, looking at his friend, much puzzled.

This was true. Dan's grandparents were away choosing shrubs for the autumn. The cousins and Uncle George were three miles downstream in their boring race. Jim had gone over to Bungay to buy himself a new jacket with the money the Vicar had given him out of 'Church Expenses'. As for the rest of the village, it was fast asleep. Dan looked ahead of him at the familiar, spilled-out bags of samples and at the rusty weighing-machine, and his courage came shakily back to him. This was Danestone in the middle of the afternoon. This was where Nick and he had played last summer. And beside him stood Henry with his bashed nose and the queer home-made patch in his jeans, regarding him with an expression of amused surprise. If he didn't pull himself together quickly, he'd be looking at him with contempt. What sort of coward was he, anyway?

'It's the old furnace house that smells so awful,' he explained quietly. 'The water's rusted the iron.'

Then he suggested that they should mount the

worn wooden stairs. The upper floor was more interesting, he said. There was a hole in the roof and one could look out through the slatted windows across the marsh. Besides, from up there they could climb the ladder on to the drying floor and see exactly where Kevin Britton had made his bed of rotten sacks.

'But for goodness sake look where you put your feet,' he warned, as his head came above the level of the floor and he could see along the dusty, worm-eaten boards. 'You don't want to fall through and bust your leg.'

Henry was as delighted with the upper gallery as Dan could possibly have wished. The light slanting through the low windows, the rough brick of the walls – even the old whiteness of the boards – were looking their very best.

'It's wonderful!' he exclaimed. 'No wonder you like it. It's like the chapel at school – except for the tiles tumbling in.'

'And look at the view,' said Dan proudly, stepping carefully towards a window. 'You can look down on the dike and the marsh. And, look! There's Uncle George's new boat-house.'

From a window at the end, he explained, you could peer through the dead elms and the willows into his grandparents' garden.

'Nick and I used to get early warning of the cousins coming,' he said with a smile.

'And you used to smoke here, too, I suppose,' remarked Henry, looking at the cigarette ends stubbed out on the window sill.

'That'll 've been Nick and Jim,' Dan replied.

'They were always escaping into the maltings to smoke.'

'Perhaps Jim does it still,' remarked Henry. 'They look quite fresh.'

It was a pity the whole place was so crazy, he thought, as he turned from the window to gaze down the long gallery again. It looked as though one good push from a strong wind would bring the whole thing down like a pack of cards.

'And now for the drying floor,' said Dan. 'Look, there's the ladder.'

And his eyes travelled slowly from its bottom-most rung up, up to a pair of dusty shoes, crumpled jeans, navy blue anorak, grey shirt, to Kevin Britton's ghastly face on top.

Dan gave a strangled cry.

The boy held a gun in his hand. It was pointed straight at Dan's head. Behind him, Henry gave a long-drawn-out sigh.

'Stay where you are,' the boy snarled, 'or I'll blow off both your heads.'

Moving his aim expertly from one to the other, he nudged them both together – as they did in American films.

'That'd be jolly stupid of you,' Henry said in an odd, croaking voice. 'They'd have you for murder.'

'So what?'

Kevin Britton looked dreadful. His face was white, his eyes huge, and he hadn't shaved for days.

'They'd . . . they'd send you down for life,' Henry said, still with an odd wobble.

'Life's only twelve years,' the boy jeered. 'If they catch me, they'll send me down for five.'

In a back corner of his mind Dan worked out that he and Henry were worth just two and a half years each. That wasn't much. But the rest of him was still appalled by the boy standing up there with his gun. He shuddered. He must have been standing there watching them all the time they had been up here on the upper floor.

'Throw it down,' said Henry more firmly.

'You bet,' Kevin snapped back viciously.

'If . . . if you fire it, you'll . . . you'll have the whole of Danestone here.'

Danestone? thought Dan. What was Henry talking about? Half the village was away. The rest was asleep. Even the hens had gone to their roosts to get out of the heat. But he must do something – say something – quickly. Henry was running out of steam.

'The police!' he suddenly blurted out. 'There's police cars going up and down the street.'

'That's your bloody fire, not me.'

'It's you all right,' said Henry, making a huge guess. 'They've come about that break-in at Thursby.'

Kevin Britton seemed to waver a second. His left arm was curiously slung across his chest with the fingers clutching his right shoulder, and with a spasm of pain he gave it a hitch.

Then his fury returned and fell upon Dan. It was all Dan's fault, he raved, that they were now at his mercy. Why had he betrayed him? Why had he come back to the maltings – and brought a stranger with him? Didn't he deserve to be shot for breaking his word?

Dan was terribly confused. All through this dreadful tirade, Henry was whispering something to him, but he couldn't hear what. Henry looked urgent, desperate, and muttered it again – and still Dan could not catch his meaning.

Then with no further warning, Henry leapt from his side to the foot of the ladder and began scrambling up its rungs.

'Hold on to the bottom,' he shouted back to Dan. 'Stop him kicking it sideways.'

Dumb with surprise, Dan did as he was told.

'I'll shoot,' screamed Kevin from overhead. 'I'll shoot. I'll shoot.'

But Henry went on disappearing up the ladder faster than ever.

Then there was a struggle and the bottom of the ladder rocked violently in Dan's frenzied grasp.

'I'll shoot,' screamed Kevin again.

And with a blinding flash, the report rocked the maltings.

'Henry,' sobbed Dan. 'Henry. Henry.'

Henry's head must be blown off. He must surely be dead.

Yet above him on the drying floor they were still fighting. And as he scrambled up the ladder after his friend to help him, Kevin began screaming with pain. When his head rose level with them, he saw that Henry was sitting on top of the boy, prising the gun out of his hand.

'My shoulder,' screamed Kevin. 'Get off my shoulder.'

'There,' said Henry, throwing the gun down on to the floor beneath. 'Now you can get up.'

But Kevin did not get up. He remained writhing on the drying tiles at their feet, clutching his left shoulder.

'I've bust my collar-bone,' he whimpered. 'I've bust it bad.'

Dan was utterly bewildered. He looked from the abject Kevin down at the gun lying on the floor below and then back to a dishevelled Henry.

Henry grinned.

'It's a starting-gun,' he said. 'I thought it might be. Then I was certain.'

'What's a starting-gun?'

'Why, for starting races, of course. Mr Bainbridge, our P.T. teacher, has one at Granthams.'

A starting-gun made a hell of a noise, he explained, but that was all. It couldn't hurt anyone. It had no bullets.

Kevin was now slowly struggling to his feet.

'Well?' he asked bitterly. 'What are you two going to do? Run home to Grandpa? Tell the police? . . .'

For all his misery, there was a seering contempt in his voice.

'. . . You'll be proper little heroes, won't you?'

The contempt shot home.

It pierced the most vulnerable chink in Dan's armour: his love for his brother Nick. Nick had done dreadful things. Not as bad as this horrible boy had done. But bad enough. And Dan had kept quiet about them. Worse still, he had covered up for his brother. Had even tried to shift the blame elsewhere. He looked at the groaning Kevin, trying to ease his left shoulder out of its pain, and felt sick at heart. This miserable thug was in a far worse position than Nick had ever been. Could he really run to the police and have him arrested? Wasn't there anyone else to get him taken away and shut up?

The contempt smashed Henry slap on the breastplate of his school honour. It put him in a terrible fix. He had been so certain what Dan ought to have done earlier when faced with Kevin. He should have told his grandfather, he had said. But now that he was faced with the runaway himself, he was torn with doubt. No Granthams boy ever split on his fellow. One bullied him instead into taking himself off to the headmaster. And wasn't this dreadful creature a boy like any other?

'You'd much better give yourself up,' he said.

It might make things easier for him, Henry suggested. They might not give him five years.

'Tell me another,' Kevin spat at him, wincing with pain as he did so.

'You'll not get far with that broken collar-bone – and without your gun.'

'There's police all over the place,' put in Dan. 'And photographs of you in the papers and descriptions of you on the radio.'

'So what?' the boy snarled. 'Now get lost both of you. I'm sick of you.'

Henry looked at his watch.

'It's ten to three,' he said. 'If you haven't given yourself up by five, we'll tell them where you are.'

They climbed down the ladder, picked up the starting-gun, and went on down to the lower floor, leaving Kevin glowering after them with his hollow, pain-ridden eyes.

In the doorway of the maltings, they stood for a moment blinking out at the glaring marsh. Both hoped that the report of the gun and the racket of the fight would have woken somebody up. But not a reed stirred. Not a murmur came to them from the direction of the village.

In the silence, they heard the boy behind them give a low laugh.

'What's he laughing for?' asked Dan, aghast.

'Don't know.'

'That motor bike? He couldn't get away on that motor bike?'

'A Suzuki 250cc? Not with a broken collar-bone. It's too heavy.'

'But he might. He *might*.'

For Dan – having heard that laugh – Kevin Britton had sprouted the horns of the Devil. And the Devil would be able to ride the Suzuki with a broken neck – let alone a mere collar-bone. He'd be up and out of Suffolk before their backs were turned.

His fear infected Henry; and they turned back into the maltings to search for the motor bike.

'But it *can't* be here!' exclaimed Henry testily, ashamed of having been over-persuaded. 'Not if he broke his collar-bone falling into that shop cellar at Thursby.'

'He could've pushed the thing back.'

'Two whole miles? Not likely.'

Then they went into the furnace room – and, tearing away the greasy sacks, found that he had.

Between them, they struggled with the Suzuki and got it out of the maltings.

'Gosh, it must've hurt him!' Dan panted, as they came out into the sunlight.

'What'll we do with it now?' asked Henry.

It seemed a thing accursed – to be got rid of as quickly as they could.

'Let it fall into the water,' suggested Dan. 'He couldn't get hold of it there.'

So they pushed it past the quay and let it topple into the head of the dike. The duck-weed opened to receive it, and the Suzuki sank gleamingly out of sight. Then they chucked Kevin's gun after it. They stood and looked down at the black hole in the weed and, while they watched, a huge bubble of mud came up from the bottom and burst with a horrible stink.

Henry looked at it uneasily.

'I don't think we ought've done that,' he said.

'Why not?'

'It belongs to someone, that Suzuki. Besides, the police'll want it for evidence.'

Well, it was too late now.

7
Tuesday Evening

THE very best-intentioned schemes sometimes go dreadfully wrong.

Dan and Henry had hardly reached home through the door in the wall when they heard Jim shouting for them from the kitchen garden. They shouted back.

'He's got his new jacket and wants to show it off,' grinned Henry, glad to push thoughts of Kevin behind him for a little.

But Jim, though certainly wearing his new jacket and mighty proud of it too, had other news to bring.

'Where ever hev yew been?' he shouted at them, as he came round the side of the house. 'We're to be up at t' Vicarage – all of us – NOW.'

'Now?' exclaimed Dan. 'But we were to meet at eight.'

All the plans had been changed, Jim gabbled. The Vicar was so pleased with the three of them, he said, and the weather was so hot that he had hired Mr Mobbs's mini-bus and was taking all the boys in the choir and themselves to the sea for a bathe and a picnic.

'Aren't we going to the fair, after all?' Dan asked.

''Corse we are.'

They were coming back to the Rushby fair straight from Cove Hythe.

'And not coming back here in between?' asked Henry.

''Corse not. Waste of petrol.'

Dan and Henry looked at each other in consternation.

Jim went on talking about the joys of the outing. Mrs Micklethwaite – who'd been cutting sandwiches for the picnic for the last hour – had said something about fish and chips for them all at Mr Balls's fish-parlour down on Rushby town quay. That was a bit of all right, now wasn't it?

'Git yer swimmin' trunks quick,' he urged.

'Henry doesn't swim,' said Dan, clutching at a straw.

'Doesn't swim?' exclaimed Jim in contemptuous disbelief. 'Well, he c'n stand and watch, c'n't he?'

'And what about Dan's grandparents and . . . and Mrs Heseltine?' asked Henry clutching at two more straws.

'Grandparents? Mrs Heseltine? What about 'em?'

'They won't know where we've gone.'

'Yew c'n write, can't yew?' Jim almost shouted at them. 'Yew c'n leave 'em a note?'

One might think that they didn't *want* to go on this wonderful treat.

'Meet you up at the Vicarage, then,' said Dan, wishing to get rid of him.

And Jim, satisfied at last, ran off home to fetch his own bathing things.

What on earth were they to do? This unexpected trip to the sea had been planned in their honour. They could not refuse to go. It would be horribly ungrateful. Besides, everyone would ask why.

'He . . . he can't get away,' began Henry hesitantly. 'Or if he does, he . . . he won't get far.'

'And if he hasn't given himself up,' said Dan, beginning to relish the joys of the North Sea. 'We can always go to the police first thing in the morning.'

Once splashing about in the waves with Jim and the choir boys, Dan forgot about Kevin. It was natural – for something wonderful was happening to him. For the first time in his life, everyone was treating him as a hero.

'Good ole Dan,' shouted Lennie Blaza, splashing him with salt water. 'He saved the church.'

'It was Jim and Henry, too,' he protested.

'Wot'd feel like fallin' through roof into ole pulpit?' asked Percy Watkin.

'Dunno,' he replied lamely. 'Rather odd, really.'

And, bursting with happiness, he dived down to the smooth-washed stones and to a rusty tin of corned beef lying on the floor of the sea. When he came up again, they were still threshing about him.

'Yew oughter gi'en a sermon, yew did,' bawled Barry Finch.

'Me text this mornin', dear fam'ly in God. . . .' boomed Reg Fairweather, taking off the Vicar.

And then, suddenly catching sight of Mr

Micklethwaite picking his way painfully over the shingle in his bare feet, they gave a shriek and dived out of sight – all at once, like a school of porpoises.

Later, striking out on his own, Dan left the choir and headed for Holland. But he gave up after a minute or two and lay floating instead on the heaving backs of the slow, grey rollers, cut off from the others, alone with the sky. Kevin came back to him then, uncomfortably at first, spoiling the joyfulness of the afternoon. What right had the horrible boy to frighten them so much and then shove all this trouble on their shoulders? The dreadful things that he had done were not their affair. Then slowly it came to him what a blessing it was that he and Henry had been whisked eight miles away by the Vicar and his picnic, for by the time that they got home tonight it would all be over. Kevin Britton would have been taken away. Nothing more need be said. No one would ever know that they'd seen him.

For Henry, left idle and alone on the beach, things were far more painful. Flashes of remembered facts from the detective stories he had been reading were beginning to reveal the full shockingness of what he and Dan had done. They had harboured a criminal – Dan had even fed him. They had destroyed evidence. They had ruined someone else's motor bike. And worse still, though appealed to by newspapers, radio, and television, they had failed to tell any of these things to the police. A dreadful phrase kept ringing in his ears: *Accessory after the Fact*. It meant that you knew a crime had been committed and that you had shielded the criminal. It was dreadful to be accessories after the fact. And that was what they were, he and Dan. Judges sometimes sent accessories to prison. In an agony of remorse he thought what this would mean to his mother; to Granthams; to himself. It would be the end of his chances of a scholarship to Winchester – for one couldn't sit for a scholarship in jail, could one? And besides, even if he won it, the school would be far too ashamed to take him.

'Yew're lookin' right dumpish,' shouted Jim, shaking salt water out of his hair as he ran past him. 'Come 'n help me get wood for t'fire.'

Henry turned in his miserable daze and saw that behind them an oak wood sprawled right down to the landward edge of the beach and that the trees nearest to the sea had been killed by the salt. Their twisted roots clutched at the sand like dead men's hands, and many of their upper branches and twigs, white and fragile in decay, had broken off and lay ready for the kindling.

'Come on! Let's make a fire,' shrieked Reg Fairweather, running up out of the sea.

'A fire! A fire!' yelled the rest of the choir, scrambling out of the languid waves and tearing past Henry in a glistening mob.

Well, a fire might cheer him up, he thought, as he slowly joined them in picking up sticks. It would at least give him something to do, something to think about other than the mess he'd made of his life.

Only Dan remained in the sea, floating far out as

innocent and oblivious as a new-sawn plank. Frightened two hours ago nearly out of his wits by Kevin and his pointing gun – and torn ever since with doubts about what the two of them had decided to do – he had now slipped into a blissful calm. Nature had made her peace with him. He was almost asleep. He thought dreamily of his new friend, Henry, and smiled and smiled. The faint awe of him that he had felt at first had quite disappeared. For Henry was just Henry. He made mistakes and contradicted himself just like anyone else. He was even frightened at times. He was sure that he had been frightened in the maltings. Lying there on top of the North Sea, gently rocking as though in a vast grey bed, Dan felt immensely grateful to Henry for not being perfect. And his mind went drifting away to Henry and himself at the fair . . . Henry and himself meeting in London . . . perhaps by some miracle even ending up at the same school.

Jim gazed up and down the beach with a puzzled look and then turned and raked the tangled oak wood.

'Where's that Dan got to?' he asked Henry.

'Don't know,' Henry replied, quickly searching the foreshore for his friend.

'He's a terror for gettin' hisself lost,' Jim burst out irritably. 'He always was.'

'We can't find Dan, Mr Micklethwaite,' shouted Lennie Blaza.

Mr Micklethwaite had come out of the water and was busy drying himself with his towel.

'I've been keeping my eye on him,' he replied

calmly. 'He's out there.'

And he pointed out to sea where Dan lay dreaming his dreams a hundred yards from the shore.

'Dan,' bawled Jim, cupping his hands into a fog horn. 'Come yew out. We're a-goin' a light t'fire.'

Dan rolled over in his bed, saw the huge pile of wood built up like a funeral pyre, and slowly made for the beach. For the moment, he felt sated with fires. Yesterday's had out-blazed Mount Etna. No fire could do better than that. But he was hungry. It was time for tea.

'I've got no matches,' muttered Jim, feeling a fool.

'Nor me.' 'Nor me,' they all wailed.

They'd been lugging that lousy old wood for nothing.

'Look in my coat pocket, Jim,' suggested the Vicar mildly, now struggling to put on his trousers.

'Can't find 'em,' said Jim, pulling out a ball of gardener's green twine, a pipe, and the crumpled proofs of the parish magazine.

'Try the other one.'

And there beneath a bag of peppermint lumps and his boy-scout whistle lay the matches.

It was an idiotic day to build a fire, thought Henry sourly. It was far too hot. Besides, it was childish. He felt angry with himself, miserable, sick at heart – and terribly confused. The Granthams code of honour had landed him slap against the law. And he didn't know where he was. With half his mind, he watched the dead wood blacken and burn, the flames almost invisible in the glaring light, and wondered if all bright things in life just turned to blackness and smoke and flying smuts like this stupid fire. And, later, when the choir of St Felix, Danestone, joined hands and danced round the pyre, shouting gibberish incantations, he wandered away disconsolately to the edge of the water, feeling a fearful gulf between himself and these savages.

Dan wandered slowly towards him with his hair sticking on end from his efforts at drying it.

'It'll be better at the fair,' he said with rare understanding. 'I'm sure it'll be better at the fair.'

It was – and it wasn't.

They ate all the sandwiches, drank all the orangeade, and bathed again. Then with the sun so low in the sky that the shadows of the dead oaks

darkened the beach, they shivered a little at the gloomy sea, and were ready to be off inland to fish-and-chips and the fair.

'Gosh! What a sky!' muttered Henry, as they drove through the flat countryside straight into the setting sun.

'It'll be dusk by the time we get to Rushby,' said Dan with a smile. 'And that's good because the fair's much more exciting at night.'

Last year he and Nick had rowed their grandparents downstream from Danestone, listening to the blare of the music from the roundabouts getting louder and louder, and turning to look over their shoulders every now and then to see the lights from the booths growing brighter and more distinct. And then, as they had approached the town quay, the river itself had become part of the fair. Between the crowded boats, the water had slapped with reflected lights. The bright blobs of the ripples and the hubbub on the quay, the whirring of the giant wheel, and the quickening pace of the merry-go-round music approaching the gallop had made Nick and himself so drunk with excitement that they had grabbed at the moorings and clambered ashore, leaving their grandparents to a swaying boat and the oars cocked up in the rowlocks.

Well, it couldn't be the same this year, he thought sadly. There was no Nick.

But there was Henry.

His new friend was muttering again in his ear.

'I won't be able to go on much,' Henry confessed. 'I've only got 20p.'

Dan rummaged in his pocket, fingering his coins.

'It's all right. I think I've got over a pound.'

Then they were on the outskirts of Rushby; and then they were driving down narrow Northgate to the quay car park.

'After fish-and-chips,' called out the Vicar, 'it's the same as last year. You all go off on your own for an hour. Enjoy yourselves. Make the most of it. Then we'll meet at the Great Wheel. Let's see, we'll make it half-past nine. Everyone got a watch? Yes? Well, don't be late – or you'll miss your free ride.'

'What's he mean?' whispered Henry.

'It's on the parish, I think,' Dan whispered back.

Henry tried to make the best of the fair. He really did. At the roundabout he chose to sit on a giant cock and, clutching its jagged red comb, shouted at Dan beside him on a dragon and tried to lose himself in the blurring fair and river and marsh as they whirled faster and faster about him. On the swings he pulled himself higher and higher into the sky, till Dan in the opposite gondola nearly fell out on the rebound. He threw balls at the coconut shies, knocked down three, and won a stupid doll. He went on the ghost-train with Dan and Jim and let himself shiver and laugh at the skeletons swinging out of the darkness and clutching at their hair. It was no good. Kevin Britton was always close beside him. Sometimes he came as a pain in the pit of his stomach, a grumbling, heavy ache like that left by the

Granthams Friday's boiled pudding; at other times, he was a huge, engulfing wave of the sea, pursuing him up over the beach and far into the oak wood. At others, he was just plain Kevin, hollow-eyed, unshaven, and laughing his horrible laugh. And at all times he knew that his whole future was at stake: that this ache, this engulfing wave, this savage boy had it in their power to ruin his chances of winning his way to Winchester.

He looked at Dan beside him, made happy and excited by the blaring music and the lights and the shouts about them, and thought: 'He's just a child, still. He doesn't realise in the least what we've done.'

Then the three of them wasted five precious pence each to see the fat lady of Lechlade, lying almost naked on a divan, smoking a hookah.

'I think they must blow her up with bicycle pumps,' whispered Dan as they left the tent.

'Garn,' replied Jim. 'It's them hormones and pills what does it. Yew c'n fatten hens w'em, so why not ladies?'

Henry was too miserable to think up how anyone could grow such mountains of pink flesh.

He looked at his watch.

'It's nearly time for the giant Wheel,' he said.

They queued for five minutes by the ticket man, waiting for the gyrating wheel to slow down and for the rest of the choir to join them, and listening to the screams of the Rushby citizens as they were spun up high to the stars at the top of the wheel and then dashed down again towards the trodden grass.

At last the thing creaked slowly to a halt, and the ticket-man, swinging each gondola in turn down to the mounting steps, released the safety bar. Down tottered the couples, two by two, pale and relieved-looking – as Noah's sea-sick passengers must have looked coming out of the ark.

'I wonder if I'm really going to like this,' Dan asked himself as he took his place beside Henry and was barred in.

Then they were swung slowly back and up as Jim took his place by Reg Fairweather in the gondola immediately below them, and then higher still as Mr Micklethwaite climbed into the next by Barry Finch. By the time that the rest of the choir had embarked Dan could look behind him and see far below the water of the cut, where the Rushby Yachting Club moored their sailing-boats, glinting red and yellow and blue from the lights of the fair.

Then with a blare from the engine's hooter, they were off up, up, up into the night and the next moment plunging down, down, down with mounting speed to the striped tents and the lights and shouts on the quay.

'It's not too bad,' Dad told himself, clutching tight to the safety bar in front of him. 'And if it gets any worse, I'll just shut my eyes.'

At the top of the wheel, anyone who cared to look could see for one dizzy instant far up the Waveney Valley away past Danestone almost to Bungay. In the darkness, there should have been nothing to see.

But there *was* something.

In the split second that their gondola swung below the stars, Henry gave a gasp of surprise. Jim, in his turn, gave a shout, and Barry Finch, poised for that instant of vision burst out:

'There's another fire, Mr Micklethwaite! Another fire over at Danestone!'

'Nonsense!' replied the Vicar. 'It's your imagination. You've all got fires on the brain.'

But as the wheel whirled them up again, first Henry and then Jim and Reg Fairweather all shouted:

'There's a fire! There's another fire!'

Mr Micklethwaite prayed hard to the Almighty, 'Not the church, please God. Not our church,' and then opened his eyes as wide as he could for his momentary glimpse up the river. There was a fire all right; but it was not stubble. It was confined to a single place; a building perhaps; not the church. And as he and Barry Finch plunged down towards the fair, he gave heartfelt thanks; he was sure it was not the church; the fire was too near the river.

'It's in Danestone Street,' Lennie Blaza bawled from the gondola above.

Round and round went the giant wheel and faster and faster, so that the scene up the river became a mere tantalizing flash. Dan could see nothing; everything to him was a sickening whirl.

'Whereabouts is it in Danestone Street?' he asked Henry.

But Henry, not truly familiar with Danestone or how it would look from the top of a giant wheel at Rushby, could not tell him.

While passing down and up through the noisy fair, Mr Micklethwaite tried to picture his beloved parish and to think how it must look from forty feet up above the Rushby quay. And when his next turn came round he strained his eyes at the pin-point of light and then shut them tight, trying to retain the image on his retina. Well, it was not the Vicarage on fire nor the Heseltines' house, nor Mr Fenton's farm. Lennie was right. The building that was blazing away was somewhere down in Danestone Street.

'This damned wheel!' he cursed under his breath. 'When is the heartless thing going to stop?'

His choirboys above and below and beside him were bumping and shouting in a fever of excitement.

'It's Mobbs's shop, I bet,' yelled Reg Fair-weather.

'What if it's the school?' laughed Jim.

'Or The Jolly Boatman,' shouted Barry Finch in triumph. 'P'raps Dad's set alight to the spirits.'

Slowly, very slowly the wheel slackened its pace and at last came to a halt with the Vicar and Barry poised at its highest point. They could stare westward now at the fire without interruption. As he did so, Mr Micklethwaite felt suddenly sick.

He looked down to find Dan. He and Henry were on a level with the tops of the booths. Neither of them could have a view up river.

'That's a blessing . . . if nothing else is,' he thought.

For he was sure that he had identified the building on fire. It was The Old House – where Dan's grandparents lived.

They were all off the great wheel as quickly as they could scramble – which was not very fast since each gondola had to be winched down in turn to the mounting steps.

'Run to the car park and the mini bus as quickly as you can,' shouted Mr Micklethwaite, suiting action to words, and sprinting off through the crowd.

As they drove out of the little town they heard a familiar quickly-jangled bell approaching from behind them and, upon Mr Micklethwaite pulling into the side of the road, they were overtaken by the Rushby fire-engine.

'I wonder whose house it is that's on fire,' said Dan.

'Your Grandad's, I think,' blurted out Barry Finch.

'Don't be a fool, boy,' rapped out the Vicar from the front. 'You don't *know*. None of us will know till we get to Danestone.'

'It may be a bonfire, sir, that's got out of control,' suggested Henry, far too promptly.

Dan felt sick. Mr Micklethwaite's sharpness and Henry hurrying in with his silly remark convinced him that they too thought that it was his grandparents' house. He peered in anguish from face to face in the darkened bus; but the faces seemed to slide away from him – as though their owners wanted no part in telling him that it was indeed so. And a great blanket of misery seemed to rise up to smother him. His grandfather. His grandmother. He loved everything about them. He loved their home, their tables and chairs, the smell of their books, the pictures on the walls, the treasures in the attic – everything that might now be going up in flames. He could not bear it. The Old House was his refuge – and Nick's refuge, too. It was a huge part of a happy past.

Guessing his distress, Henry pressed his hand. And Dan, looking up at his friend, suddenly remembered something that they had both heard only that afternoon. It was something so terrible that it made him shudder. It was Kevin Britton's fiendish laugh. Was it possible that he had taken his revenge out on his poor grandparents?

Though Mr Micklethwaite jammed down the accelerator so that the old bus shook to its bones, the two miles to Danestone had never seemed so long. But at last they were hurtling past the end of Church Lane and The Jolly Boatman and Mobbs's shop.

And suddenly a great shout went up.

'It's all right, Dan,' burst out the Vicar, almost laughing with relief. 'Your grandparents are quite safe.'

It was not The Old House that was on fire. It was the maltings.

The bus came to a grinding halt outside the primary school, and Mr Micklethwaite and his choir scrambled out and ran down Fenton's Lane towards the blaze. The whole village was gathered at the head of the dike, standing there in a human wall, black against the towering flames, while ahead of them the jets of water from the firemen's hoses were just beginning to play on to the burning roof.

'It's a sad end to the old place,' said a familiar voice, and Mr Fenton's face turned for a moment and was caught in the light.

'Nonsense,' replied Colonel Henchman sharply. 'You should have pulled it down years ago.'

Dan took one look over the grown-ups heads at the lurid smoke pouring out of the top of the pagoda chimney and was seized by a new and quite different terror.

'It's lucky it's just the old maltings and that there's no one inside it,' he heard Mrs Micklethwaite say to his grandmother.

And, impelled by his terror, he was off kicking and pushing his way forward through the legs of the people of Danestone. That awful boy, he thought. He's caught inside. He's asleep. He's ill. He's bust his collar-bone. I can't leave him there.

'Hallo, Dan,' he heard Simon say as he jostled past. 'You're late. You've missed the best part.'

But he was out now by the firemen, leaping over the bulging hoses, tripping, falling, but up again, making straight for the door into the maltster's den.

'Dan, Dan,' he heard behind him. 'Come back. Dan! Dan!'

As he reached the threshold a great flurry of smoke burst out from the lower floor, choking and blinding him. He paused for a moment – and in that moment someone caught him in an iron vice.

'Dan! Dan!' roared his grandfather. 'What the hell are you at?'

'He's in there,' he screamed, struggling to get free.

'Who's in there?' shouted his grandfather, hurting him badly as he hauled him back towards the fire-engine.

'Kevin Britton,' he sobbed. 'The boy they're all looking for.'

'Get away, sir,' yelled one of the firemen. 'Get the boy right away. She's coming down. The roof's giving way.'

And hardly had he spoken when a great rending of split rafters joined the roar of the flames. His grandfather gave him a final, savage tug and flung him into the nettles beside the upturned boat. Dan, lying there crying, saw beyond the panting, exhausted old man, the crazy maltings come to their final end. With a slither of pantiles, the roof fell in, the walls bulged out, and in a smother of dust and smoke and falling bricks, the joyful place of his childhood – his and Nick's – settled flat and quite useless like a house made of cards. He sobbed and sobbed not for the past but for the boy – the horrible boy – who must be dead or dying under all the rubble.

The end of the maltings was so sudden and so awe-inspiring that it struck the people of Danestone quite dumb. They stood there without a word massed at the head of the dike, listening to the faint swish of the hoses playing over the smouldering bricks, to Dan's smothered weeping, and to the huge silence of the marsh that lay beyond the crumbled building.

Then an unmistakable sound caught their ears: the engine of a speed-boat starting up. They listened more intently. Whoever it was farther down the dike was in a tremendous hurry. The engine was screaming like a cat.

'Someone's stolen Dad's speed-boat,' yelled Nigel.

'Get up,' said his grandfather sternly to Dan still lying in the nettles. 'Get yourself through the fence into the garden. I'll be with you as soon as I can.'

8

The Reckoning

'You found him there on *Saturday morning*' his grandfather rounded on him once they were back in his study.

Dan glanced up from the carpet at the angry old man and felt hopelessly unfit for what was to come.

'Yes,' he muttered.

'Then why *on earth* didn't you tell us?'

'Because I th . . . thought . . . I thought he'd just run away.'

'Nonsense. You were afraid. You were afraid I'd be angry with you for breaking your promise.'

'Yes,' replied Dan wildly. 'No. . . . Yes.'

Whenever grown-ups stormed at him he lost his head.

'Come on, Dan. Which was it?'

'I . . . I don't know,' he stammered, fighting back his tears. He felt miserable. The nettles throbbed like bee-stings. The Cove Hythe sand in his shoes felt like ground glass. And his grandfather thought him a liar. A coward.

Someone slipped into the room behind him, and his grandfather looked up.

'Dan knew all about the boy, Madge. He found him in the maltings on Saturday morning.'

'On Saturday morning?' exclaimed his grandmother. 'But Dan, that was the very first day of your visit!'

Whenever it was, thought Dan in his wretchedness, it seemed ages ago to him. What happened in such a distant past really shouldn't count any more.

'But on Monday morning,' pursued his grandfather without mercy '. . . when the boy's picture appeared in the papers and you knew that he was wanted by the police, didn't it occur to you even *then* that you ought to tell us both?'

'I . . . I thought he'd gone. He . . . he promised he'd go on Saturday night.'

'And you believed him?'

'Yes.'

Dan was quite certain about that.

'You were a fool. What does a boy like that know about keeping his word?'

'Well, Roland dear,' put in his grandmother mildly. 'The boy would have been very hungry. He'd have to leave the maltings to get something to eat.'

'So he raided the shop at Thursby,' rapped out his grandfather. 'That poor Mrs Mavers can thank *you* for that, Dan.'

Dan couldn't see the logic of this. But then his mind was in a great turmoil in his fear for what was to come next.

But for the moment the worst charge of his guilt didn't come, for his grandmother, inconsequent as ever, wandered off up a side road.

'It's very strange,' she said thoughtfully.

'Friday night . . . all Saturday . . . how did the boy manage for something to drink? He must have been dying of thirst.'

He couldn't have drunk water out of the dike, she said. It was too foul. And there was no rain-water butt in the maltings as far as she could remember.

'It doesn't matter does it?' snapped his grandfather impatiently. 'He managed. And that's that.'

'I gave him a bottle of milk,' said Dan, looking at his grandmother. He couldn't bear for her not to know the truth. 'I'm sorry. I took it off the kitchen window-sill.'

'You did *what*?' roared his grandfather.

'And . . . I gave him something . . . something out of your freezer.'

Dan continued to speak only to his grandmother. He was repaying her a debt.

'Oh, Dan dear,' she smiled weakly. 'What a funny thing to do.'

'*Funny?*' barked the ex-magistrate. 'It's out-rageous! – Aiding and abetting a criminal by stealing from one's grandparents? Do you call that *funny?*'

'No, it isn't, dear. I know it isn't. But look at him. He's only a child.'

His grandfather looked at him – and then snorted.

'You're eleven, aren't you?'

Dan agreed reluctantly that he was.

'Then you are old enough to have had more sense. You're not a fool.'

In the silence that followed Dan tried to gather his wits together for the next question that his grandfather was surely going to ask him: *why did you think that Kevin Britton was still in the maltings tonight?* It was coming. It was coming, he thought in anguish, as he watched the bushy brows knit and the angry eyes rake his face again.

But instead, all that came was a knock at the study door.

'We're busy,' shouted his grandfather.

The newcomer, taking no notice, opened the door, and Dan, turning round saw Henry looking white-faced but resolute.

'You, Henry?' exclaimed his grandfather frowning. 'Why aren't you back with the Heseltines and in bed?'

'Because I ought to be here, sir.'

'No, boy, we'll see you tomorrow,' said the old man, rising to show him the door. 'This is a family affair.'

'And I'm part of it, sir.'

Henry explained. He gave his story with the crispness of a junior officer making a report to a general. It had been *his* fault, he said. All his fault. He knew that Dan was forbidden to go into the maltings, but he had bullied and jeered at him this morning until he had given in. The two of them had taken their chance in the afternoon.

'While you, sir, and Mrs Henchman were over at Loddon.'

'Quite a carefully-planned operation,' commented Dan's grandfather drily.

Henry flushed.

'And we found him there,' burst in Dan, 'waiting for us up on the drying-floor. He'd got a gun.'

'A *gun*!' exclaimed his grandmother in horror. 'What ever did you do?'

'Shouted to him to throw it down . . . but he wouldn't.'

'And what then?' asked his grandfather.

'He started yelling at me and saying dreadful things . . . and then Henry kept saying something . . . but I couldn't hear what . . . and then . . . then he rushed up the ladder.'

'Who did?'

'Henry, of course,' rapped out Dan impatiently. 'And then . . . then he got to the top and he grabbed him and . . . and the gun went off.'

'Good heavens!' exclaimed both his grandparents at once.

'Do you mean you tackled him while he was pointing a gun at you?' his grandfather asked Henry.

'Oh no, sir. It wasn't like that,' said Henry, blushing painfully. 'It wasn't like that at all. It was a starting-gun. While he was shouting at Dan and waving the gun at him I took a good look at it. I knew it was only a starting-gun before I climbed the ladder.'

Besides, he explained, he had also seen that the boy had hurt himself in some way.

'He bust his collar-bone falling into Mrs Mavers's cellar,' Dan said.

'Goodness!' sighed his grandmother faintly, sitting down on a chair. 'And all the time we were buying shrubs in Loddon!'

His grandfather looked first at Henry and then at Dan.

'And what did you do with the boy then?' he asked, smiling his strange lop-sided smile.

'We . . . we threw the gun down on to the floor below and then . . . and then we made him promise to give himself up.'

'*Promise?*' exploded his grandfather, angry again. 'You fools! But Kevin Britton doesn't keep his promises. Dan, you'd already learnt that for yourself.'

'We gave him two hours,' explained Henry. 'We told him that if he didn't give himself up by five o'clock, then *we'd* go to the police. You see, sir, he was done for. He couldn't get far with a broken collar-bone and no gun and no motor bike.'

'No motor bike?'

'We found it in the furnace room,' said Dan. 'So we pushed it in the dike . . . and chucked the gun in after it.'

'My God,' groaned Colonel Henchman. 'How on earth am I going to explain *that* to the police?'

'And after that, Dan, dear,' said his grandmother vaguely, 'you and Henry went off on the choir outing. Is that right?'

In the silence that followed they looked at the carpet feeling infinitely foolish.

'We . . . we didn't know what else to do,' Dan stammered out lamely.

'And in the meantime,' rasped his grandfather, 'Kevin Britton set fire to Mr Fenton's maltings and made his get-away in your Uncle George's speedboat!'

Well, he said, as he sent Henry back to the Heseltines and Dan off to bed, there'd be the devil to pay tomorrow when the police heard what they had done. He'd do his best for them – but they had behaved like a couple of fools.

'There's one good thing,' he said in conclusion. 'There's not a ghost of a chance that the boy'll get away. The river police have been called out on patrol. Your Uncle George has seen to that. There's no cover on a river. He'll be picked up in a matter of hours.'

His grandmother, however, was taking no chances. She refused to allow Dan to sleep out in the summer-house.

'I don't trust that boy,' she said darkly as she bundled him up to a much needed bath. 'Or the wits of the river police, either. You'll sleep safe and sound upstairs in your old room. And we'll lock the front door.'

Dan was silently thankful.

Later, lying in his bed next to Nick's empty one, he felt utterly exhausted by the day's mishaps. Still, he thought sleepily, the worst was over. His grandfather now knew all that there was to know. Tomorrow surely could not be as bad.

'Dan,' said his grandmother shyly when she came in to tuck him up. 'I . . . I think I understand. Whatever happens tomorrow with the police, I'd like you to know that I understand.'

Did she really, he wondered. He hardly understood himself.

'He's dead,' she whispered. 'Nick's dead. You don't have to protect him any more.'

And she turned out his light.

Was that it? Was it as easy as that?

By the door, she stopped and gave a little laugh.

'I'm so glad you told me about the milk bottle,' she said. 'I get so forgetful these days . . . and I thought that my memory was at fault.'

Next morning Dan awoke late to the sunlight streaming through the crack in the curtains and, finding himself in a proper bed with a white ceiling staring down on him, he remembered all that had happened the day before.

Well, it was all over, he thought with a comfortable sigh of relief. The police did not matter very much now that his grandfather had been told. Besides, unless Kevin Britton had been caught and had blabbed, they need not know anything about Henry and himself. The whole matter could be forgotten. Swept under the carpet.

His hopes, however, were rudely shattered at breakfast. The telephone bell rang and his grandfather answered it from the extension on the kitchen dresser.

'Colonel Henchman? Yes, Colonel Henchman speaking,' he said. 'Yes, Inspector, what can I do for you? . . .'

Dan finished the cornflakes in his mouth as quietly as he could.

'You've caught him? . . . Down at Burgh St Peter? . . . Well done. . . . What's that? . . . Good

Lord! . . . Completely smashed up? . . . I'm sorry about that. . . .'

The voice on the other end of the telephone talked on and on, while Dan and his grandmother exchanged glances. Was it Kevin Britton who was 'completely smashed up'? Or another policeman? . . . Or Uncle George's fabulous new speedboat?

'A small boy with glasses?' barked Dan's grandfather. 'Yes. That's my grandson. . . . Where is he? Why here, sitting beside me eating his breakfast. . . . Yes. . . . Yes. . . . Very well, Inspector. We'll expect you.'

He replaced the telephone, turned back to his bacon and eggs, and went on eating – quickly and fiercely, as though he were in camp and a battle was about to begin.

'What is it, dear?' asked Dan's grandmother.

They had caught the little wretch, he snapped out between mouthfuls, but not before he had rammed George's precious speedboat slap into Burgh Staithe. The fibreglass had split from end to end and its £1000 engine was now sitting ten feet deep in the mud.

'And the boy?'

'Oh, they fished him out of the river, all right. He's in poor shape, they say. But it hasn't prevented him from talking.'

'About me?' asked Dan.

'About you,' barked his grandfather angrily. 'And about Henry, too. Inspector Phillips will be over from Rushby in twenty minutes to get a statement from you both.'

✴ ✴ ✴

164

Oh, goodness, thought Dan wearily half an hour later. How grown-ups do go on and on! He had told his story to his grandfather last night. He had already told it all over again to this inspector from Rushby and now he was being asked to tell it a *third* time, in short, tidy sentences so that the inspector could write it down. And the more he told it the sillier it sounded. He was heartily sick of the whole thing.

'Wake up, Dan,' his grandfather barked. 'The inspector wants you to tell him once again why you failed to tell the police that you had found Kevin Britton in the maltings yesterday afternoon.'

'Because . . . because we thought he'd get a lighter sentence if . . . if he gave himself up. And . . . and we thought he couldn't get away not with his broken collar-bone and . . . and no gun.'

'Wait a minute . . . not so fast.'

'We . . . we didn't think of the speedboat. . . .'

Why should they have done? Only he and Nick had known how to break into the boat-house. And it came to him at last that Kevin must have been standing at one of the maltings' windows on Saturday morning watching how he had dived under the water-gate and unlocked it from the inside.

'. . . We only thought of the motor cycle. And . . . and to stop him using that . . . we threw it in the dike.'

Well, it was over at last and he signed the boring thing and went out to the kitchen where he found Henry looking as though he had not slept for a week.

His grandfather followed him out of the study.

'Your turn next, Henry,' he said curtly. 'But first I must tell you your rights. Before making a statement, you can either ask for a solicitor or for your mother to be present.'

'My mother?' exclaimed Henry, appalled.

'In Dan's case – since I'm his grandfather – I stood in as one of his parents. Shall I ask the inspector if I can do the same for you? We're old friends in administering the law in these parts.'

'Yes please, sir.'

'First though, tell me, have you told the Heseltines of your part in this affair?'

Henry blushed furiously.

'No, sir. Should I have?'

'Thank God for that! You've got some sense after all.'

'Can I come with you?' asked Dan, as they were about to go.

'Of course not.'

'Why not?'

'The inspector has heard your story. Now he wants to hear Henry's.'

'Doesn't he think I told the truth?'

'It's not that, dear,' said his grandmother, smiling faintly. 'It's just the way the law works. Besides, I think . . . I think there's more than one kind of truth, don't you?'

And Dan had to be content with that for the endless half hour in which he waited for Henry to come out of the study.

Henry came out looking as though he had been dredged up from a very deep pool. The inspector had asked what school he attended and, on being told, had snapped back that an expensive private education had not taught him very much. And Henry had felt dreadfully upset and confused because it was precisely what Granthams had taught him that had made him give Kevin Britton a final chance.

He looked wanly at Dan.

'We've got to show him where in the dike we threw the bike and the gun,' he muttered.

'That's easy,' said Dan, trying to cheer him up. 'There'll be a great, black hole in the duck-weed.'

His grandfather made them take the inspector out through the kitchen garden to avoid passing through half the village which was crowding round the flashing police-car drawn up outside the front gate.

'We'll send our divers out this afternoon, Colonel,' said the inspector after he had inspected the hole.

Thank goodness it was that particular Wednesday in August! It was the last day of the Regatta. And at 12.30 all the young people of Danestone fought their way on to the Rushby bus, hell-bent on watching the swimming sports in the town pool and then roughing up the fair. When the police van arrived with the divers, the street was deserted. Close behind it came a break-down lorry equipped with a winch – a strange cavalcade, indeed, to be seen turning down over-grown Fenton's Lane.

Henry and Dan sat on the garden railings

overlooking the head of the dike, with Dan's grandparents standing behind them in the long grass, and watched the young policemen disappear into the back of the van and reappear minutes later in their wet suits, dangling their snorkels.

'Now, lads,' said their leader. 'Show us exactly where you pushed it in.'

And the two boys jumped down and showed them.

Down went the divers and, with the plopping of the water, up came the dreadful stink of the mud.

'You might've chosen somewhere cleaner,' groaned the policeman in charge. 'This must be the Danestone sewer.'

'Nonsense, Constable,' barked Dan's grandfather, who had climbed over the railings and joined them. 'We're all on main drains.'

'Look!' shouted Dan.

Up out of the filth had shot a hand holding Kevin's gun; and a moment later up came the rest of the diver.

'We've found them both,' he spluttered in triumph. 'The gun on top of the bike. Get the winch round here. We'll get her out in minutes.'

'Thank God for that!' thought Henry, who wanted the whole horrible thing over and done with and the last of Kevin Britton smuggled quickly out of Danestone. The marsh was empty. There was no one about. If only the policemen didn't shout too much, no one in the village need know what they were hauling up out of the dike. No one except the policemen and Dan's grandparents need know what fools he and Dan had been.

But it was not to be.

In the silence, while the policeman went to attend to the winch, came a soft, rhythmic dipping sound from farther down the dike.

'What's that?' he asked sharply.

'Someone rowing up from the river,' replied Dan, gazing short-sightedly over the heap of blackened bricks which had once been the maltings and listening attentively to the slow dipping of the oars. 'He's not in a hurry.'

Slowly, very slowly over the top of the bank, Jim's head appeared, then his back, and – at last – as he turned the slight bend in the dike, the prow of his Uncle Ed's old rowing-boat. On he came, stroke after slow stroke with his back to them, getting closer and closer. Then one of the policemen shouted an order to the man with the winch, and Jim turned round and saw them.

He stared first at the policemen and then at Henry and Dan and Dan's grandparents and then grew scarlet in the face with embarrassment. With the sure instinct of the born wrong-doer, he knew that he had caught his friends out in some sort of guilt.

'They're pulling out Kevin Britton's motor bike,' blurted out Dan. 'It got thrown into the dike.'

Jim shipped his oars, hitched the painter of the boat round a rotting bollard on the old maltings' quay, and came and stood beside them as the winch slowly dragged Trevor Fincher's mud-

clogged Suzuki back up into the light of day.

'Cor, thet en't half in a mess!' he exclaimed as the motor cycle was swung dripping on to the village staithe. 'It'll cost a mint to put right.'

'Will it really?' gasped Henry, turning distraught to Dan's grandfather.

The old man looked at him, his fierce glance slowly softening. Then, unbelievably, he brushed the whole matter aside as if of no importance. Things happened when there were boys about, he said. He was used to that.

'In fact, Henry,' he added with a wry smile. 'I've seriously thought of insuring myself against the summer holidays.'

'And Mr Heseltine's new speedboat?' Henry asked, still taut with the consequences of what he and Dan had done.

'Oh, there are no flies on my son-in-law,' replied the Colonel drily. 'Everything he possesses is insured up to the hilt.'

Jim, listening to what was being said, looked from Henry and the Colonel back to Dan, standing by his grandmother watching the Suzuki disappearing inside the police van, and guessed to a 't' what had really happened.

When the Rushby police had gone, Dan's grandfather turned to him.

'And why aren't you at the fair with the others?' he asked.

Jim looked embarrassed again. He had come with an offer. But now at the last moment he was afraid how it was going to be received.

'Seein' as how yew've no row boat this summer,' he muttered. 'I was . . . I was wonderin'. . . .'

'If we could all row down to the fireworks in your Uncle Ed's!' burst in Dan, overjoyed that their annual treat need not be foregone.

'Thet's it,' said Jim, kicking at the grass on the overgrown staithe.

'That's very kind of you, Jim,' said Dan's grandfather, visibly touched. The old family rowing-boat had finally rotted away in the winter months. And after Nick's death he had not found the heart to buy another. 'What do you say, Madge?'

'And Jim and I can do the rowing,' gabbled Dan.

Only Henry still looked miserable.

'Cheer up, Henry,' laughed Dan's grandmother. 'We'll wrap you up in life-belts.'

One more black hour still had to be lived through.

When they returned to The Old House, they heard the telephone bell ringing. It was the Rushby inspector to say that the detective inspector from Wellingborough who was in charge of the Britton case had now arrived at the police station and wished to interview the two boys.

'Will he charge us with being accessories?' asked Henry as Dan's grandfather drove them into the little town.

'Shouldn't think so,' replied the old man.

'We shan't have to tell our stories all over again, shall we?' sighed Dan.

The whole affair was behind him, now that his grandfather knew all about it. It was finished. A lesson learnt. A bore. The police were just inquisitive outsiders.

'They've got your statements.'

'Then why do they want to see us?' asked Henry.

'At worst it'll be a caution,' said the Colonel. 'At best it'll be a round ticking off. He'll tell you once again what a couple of damned fools you've been.'

'A caution doesn't sound very awful,' said Dan, almost cheerfully.

But there he was wrong, his grandfather corrected him. A caution was a very serious and formal affair. It was the next worst thing to a charge. And it went down on one's file.

'Have Henry and I got files?' Dan asked in wonder.

It sounded as though they were both in a spy story.

'No. No minor has a file until the police give him a caution. Then it goes down on a file – and the next time he's in trouble with the law, he's for it.'

'I see,' said Henry very quietly.

Well, it was a sharp reprimand not a caution. A citizen's duty, they were told, was to help and inform the police, not to take the law into his own hands. Childish ideas of 'giving second chances' and 'fair play' did not work when dealing with violent young people like Kevin Britton. Next time they must tell all they knew to the authorities, not try to tackle the criminal on their own.

'And . . . and our statements?' Henry asked, as they were dismissed.

'We'll keep them,' they were told. But it was most unlikely that they would hear anything more about them. The young thug had caused quite enough mischief without it being necessary to implicate two silly young boys who should have known better.

Henry emerged into the hot glare of the police yard, feeling humbled and bruised – and yet wonderfully delivered from sin. Christian's burden had gone rolling down a mountainside.

Dan's thoughts had shot ahead to happier things.

'And now for tonight – and the fireworks,' he said with a grin.

Ed Foulger's rowing-boat glided down the Waveney with the last light of the August day dying out in the sky behind it and the darkness ahead thickening from the east over Rushby, its five occupants marvellously at peace with one another and with the quiet world slipping slowly upstream on either side. For Henry, bulky in a life-jacket seated on the floor-boards between Dan's grandparents' feet, the long worry was over. He was reprieved. Better still, he felt accepted. He looked at Dan in front of him, so unexpectedly deft in handling his oar, and at the dark form of Jim handling his behind him and knew he was happier in his friends than he had been for weeks. From above him came the male smell of tobacco smoke and, looking up, he saw the faint glow of the Colonel's pipe. Beside him sat Dan's grandmother with the rudder-ropes in her hands, steering them into the darkness. He sighed with happiness. It was all so quiet and ordinary and unfussed. And – for this one night at least – he belonged. For Jim, rowing Dan and his grandparents and Dan's friend Henry down to the fireworks, things were much simpler. He was remembering Nick – and remembering his friend in the best way he could think of. As for Dan, watching the dark water open to his oar and then slip away quietly upstream, he was content – and much more than content – at the way things had turned out. In the last five days he had been greatly frightened, had behaved like a fool, and had even told lies. Yet his grandparents had forgiven him – and he had gained two friends.

'Look!' exclaimed his grandmother. 'Look! The first rocket!'

And Dan and Jim swivelled round on their seats to watch a thrown handful of coloured stars slowly drifting down through the darkness.

'We must hurry! Hurry!' exclaimed Dan, turning back to grab his oar.

'No need,' said the Colonel quietly. 'The tide'll take us. Besides, we're almost there.'

The silent drifting of the old boat on the strong ebb tide seemed magical to Henry. Without sound and without effort, they glided between the houses and under the old railway bridge and among the darkened boats into a night shot with stars and bearded comets and whirling, brilliant showers while the reports of the fireworks ricocheted over the water like sharp gunfire.

'Poor old Simon and Nigel,' he thought. 'Shut up in that boring old Yacht Club.'

'Well, this is a happier good-night,' said Dan's grandmother as she tucked him up in bed that night.

'Yes. Yes. It is,' he agreed. 'But. . . .'

'But what?'

'It's . . . it's about Henry. . . .'

'What about Henry?'

'I . . . I like him so much and . . . and I shan't ever see him again when he goes home next week.'

'Goodness! Why not? You both live in London.'

'But . . . but he goes to a much grander school than I do.'

'That hasn't made any difference between you both while you've been down here, has it?'

'No.'

'Then, it's quite simple. When your father and mother come home from Switzerland, we'll ask them if Henry can spend the Christmas holidays with you.'

'Is that all right?' he asked, smiling.

'Of course it's all right. He'll like it as much as you do.'

She did not add that it might save poor Henry from another disastrous visit to her other grandsons. Instead, she kissed Dan good-night and turned out the light.

'And tomorrow,' he said sleepily. 'Can I go back to the summer-house?'

'Of course.'